**"What was cause of death?" Macy asked.**

"Puncture wounds and scoring on the bone indicate he was stabbed multiple times. Judging from the size and length of the scoring, it could have been done by a hunting knife or a common kitchen knife," the ME responded.

Which her mother could have grabbed in the house. Macy remembered that one of the knives was missing when she was taking inventory of the kitchen. Remembered seeing an image of blood trickling down her arm...

"Evidence suggests he was killed at least two decades ago, maybe twenty-five to twenty-seven years," the ME continued.

Macy rubbed her temple and sighed.

Stone gave her a sympathetic look. "You okay?"

She shook her head, her eyes pained. "If he's been dead that long and in that wall the whole time, my mother and I would have been living there."

Stone swallowed. He saw the wheels in her head spinning. If what she said was true, Macy's mother might know exactly what had happened.

Or...she might have murdered the man herself.

# THE BODY IN THE WALL

USA TODAY Bestselling Author

RITA HERRON

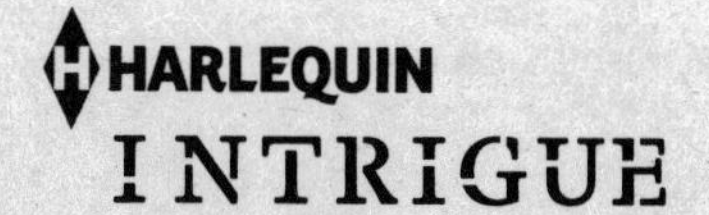

To my fabulous and very patient editor, Allison Lyons!

Thanks for always supporting me!

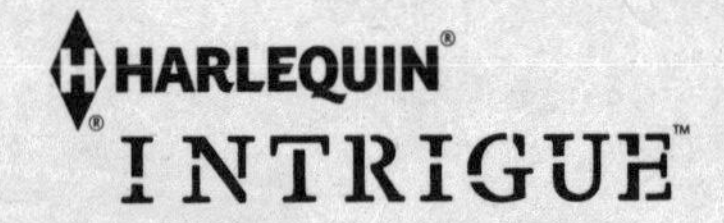


ISBN-13: 978-1-335-48960-9

The Body in the Wall



Harlequin Enterprises ULC
22 Adelaide St. West, 41st Floor
Toronto, Ontario M5H 4E3, Canada
www.Harlequin.com

**Printed in U.S.A.**

*USA TODAY* bestselling author **Rita Herron** wrote her first book when she was twelve but didn't think real people grew up to be writers. Now she writes so she doesn't have to get a real job. A former kindergarten teacher and workshop leader, she traded storytelling to kids for writing romance, and now she writes romantic comedies and romantic suspense. Rita lives in Georgia with her family. She loves to hear from readers, so please visit her website, ritaherron.com.

**Books by Rita Herron**

**Harlequin Intrigue**

***A Badge of Courage Novel***

*The Secret She Kept*
*The Body in the Wall*

***A Badge of Honor Mystery***

*Mysterious Abduction*
*Left to Die*
*Protective Order*
*Suspicious Circumstances*

***Badge of Justice***

*Redemption at Hawk's Landing*
*Safe at Hawk's Landing*
*Hideaway at Hawk's Landing*
*Hostage at Hawk's Landing*

*Cold Case at Camden Crossing*
*Cold Case at Carlton's Canyon*
*Cold Case at Cobra Creek*
*Cold Case in Cherokee Crossing*

Visit the Author Profile page at Harlequin.com.

## CAST OF CHARACTERS

***Sheriff Stone Lawson***—He swore to protect the town. But can he save the woman he loves from a killer?

***Special Agent Macy Stark***—Did her mother kill Voight Hubert and hide his body in the wall of Macy's childhood home?

***Lynn Stark***—Macy's mother has a mental illness. But is she a murderer?

***Voight Hubert***—The dead man in the wall was a hired killer. But who hired him?

***Angie Wilkins***—Voight Hubert attacked her years ago. Did her father kill him?

***Prentice Walkman***—Is the senatorial candidate the honest man he claims to be?

***Adeline Walkman***—How far will she go to protect her husband's secrets?

# *Chapter One*

Sheriff Stone Lawson sank into his desk chair and stared at the letter marked "To My Older Self." Yesterday at the reunion, he'd opened the time capsule and found the notes his classmates had written themselves, predicting where they thought they'd be years after graduation.

In his, he'd vowed to follow in his father's footsteps and work in law enforcement. He thought he'd probably get married and have a bunch of boys, his own football team in the making.

But that had all changed the day of the shooting. The day his little brother, Mickey, had been partially blinded by a bullet.

Stone's hands bunched into fists. He was the older brother. He should have protected him.

Guilt thundered through his chest every time he saw or talked to Mickey. They'd grown up roughhousing, diving off the ridges into the river in the mountains, pranking each other. Playing football. Hiking and fishing.

Then Mickey's future had been interrupted.

He closed his eyes, the image of his injured brother

fighting for his life fifteen years ago taunting him. He swallowed back the pain, then opened his eyes and called Mickey's number. When he didn't answer, worry nagged at him. He hoped to hell his brother wasn't already three sheets to the wind. Mickey had been drinking way too much lately.

His deputy poked his head in. "Sheriff, Hazel LeCroy just called. Said someone just broke into the pawnshop. Stole a gun."

Someone stealing guns couldn't be good.

He found his deputy Murphy Bridges in the break room and told him where he was going, then headed outside to his police-issued SUV. His gut burned with a bad feeling.

There had been protestors against the new school Kate McKendrick had lobbied for. People in town blaming each other for what had happened. Although the new school was under way and a memorial had been built for the students lost that fateful day. And he and Special Agent Macy Stark, another former student, had finally discovered the reason behind the shooting and who had given Ned Hodgkins the gun—Macy's ex.

What if the recent publicity surrounding the shooting had triggered enough anger and emotion to cause someone to retaliate? Or another student to want the attention Ned had received?

SPECIAL AGENT MACY STARK had dreaded this moment for years. Had vowed never to return to her childhood home in Briar Ridge, North Carolina.

The night of graduation she'd packed her bags

and run away the next morning. Her mother had still been in bed, so doped up on meds that she probably hadn't realized her daughter was gone for days.

Guilt for leaving her had nagged at Macy as she'd boarded the bus out of town, but her mother had abandoned her so many times, even the night of the shooting when Macy had been traumatized, that she'd had to go or she'd literally drown in depression.

With her mother in a long-term treatment facility, she was only here to clean out the house now and get it on the market. Then she'd go back to her life and try to put the past behind her.

But her phone buzzed and her ex-husband's number appeared on the screen. She'd arrested Trey a few days ago for supplying Ned Hodgkins with the gun he'd used to slaughter the students at Briar Ridge High fifteen years ago. But the DA had thrown out the charges, saying they had no proof that Trey knew Ned's intentions.

She let the call go to voice mail, knowing it was probably another irate message from Trey threatening to get back at her for humiliating him in front of the town. All she wanted to do was be done with him, just as she wanted to do with her childhood home.

The old house had been run-down when she'd lived here, but it was nothing compared to the state it was in now. Dust motes hung heavy in the musty air. The once-white walls had faded to yellow, the paint was chipped and battered, and the wood floor was scratched. The linoleum in the tiny kitchen that her mother had never used was lifting in places and was a nasty pea-green shade scarred with cigarette burns where her mother had dropped lit cigarettes when she was stumbling around, incapacitated.

Macy had had to stomp them out several times. Her senior year on Thanksgiving, she'd woken up and smelled smoke. When she'd tiptoed into the den, she'd found her mother passed out on the couch. Smoke was seeping from the vinyl couch cushions. She'd dragged her mother off the couch, then dumped water on the sofa until she doused the fire starting to shoot from the bottom.

That orange vinyl monstrosity still sat against the wall, tattered, soot-stained and reeking of smoke. Swallowing against the emotions churning through her, she flipped on a lamp and noted the place was piled high with clutter. Old magazines were stacked waist-deep by the woodburning fireplace, along with boxes of junk items that must have come from the thrift store, a fire hazard in the making. The rocking chair in the corner needed re-caning, and one of the legs on the old maple table in the kitchen was broken, making the table slant sideways. The scent of dirt, cigarette smoke and mildew permeated the walls, and the kitchen counter and stove were scarred and stained, sticky clumps of something smeared on the surfaces. Ants congregated along the edge of the rotting windowsill, and dead fruit flies dotted the counter.

Bile rose to her throat. How had her mother lived like this?

A rotten odor wafted toward her as she neared the refrigerator, and she held her breath as she eased open the door and looked inside. Except for condiments she was sure were outdated, it was bare, a sign her mother had been gone for months. In the freezer, Macy found a butcher-wrapped package of some kind of meat that was covered in frost it was so old.

Closing the door, she decided to tackle cleaning it out later. First, she had to assess the gravity of the job. Maybe she should hire someone to clean out the place so she wouldn't have to spend more time in this disaster.

The sound of her mother's shrill voice echoed in Macy's ears as she walked down the hall to the bedrooms. Everything looked older and dusty, but her mother had not changed anything, as if she'd expected Macy to one day return and for them to be a happy, smiling family.

They never had been, though. She'd given up that fantasy a long time ago.

The faded yellow bedspread remained; her childhood teddy bear sat on the bookshelf along with a rag doll and the river rocks she'd collected when she'd bypassed the doll stage. She gasped, though, as she surveyed the walls. She'd never hung posters of rock bands or movie stars. Instead, she'd idolized track stars and had taped posters of the high school team on the wall above the knotty pine desk.

Those posters were gone now, scattered on the floor in shreds as if her mother had ripped them apart in a fit of rage.

Maybe at that point she'd given up on Macy coming home.

A clap of thunder burst outside, and through the

window, lightning zigzagged across the darkening sky, catapulting Macy back in time to that night when she was five.

*It was storming outside. Macy hated storms. The loud booming frightened her, and the lightning flashes lit up the dark woods where the monsters hid. Except sometimes at night when her mother locked her in her room, Macy thought those monsters sneaked inside.*

*Tonight, she heard one of them. Boots pounding. The floor creaking. Cold air wafting through the eaves of the thin walls. Thunder mingling with other noises. Furniture being knocked over. Her mother's shrill cry. The basement door squeaking open...*

*The basement...it was off-limits. Scary dark. Her mother told her the monsters would get her if she went down there.*

*Macy believed her.*

*So why was her mother opening the door? Why was she going down there tonight?*

*Terrified, Macy crept to the door and listened. Another scream. Some grunting sound. More thunder. She covered her ears with her hands and pressed down hard to drown out the sound.*

*She pushed her bedroom door open slightly and peeked through the crack. Suddenly her mother jerked the door open. Her hair was a tangled mess, her eyes wide, her breath puffing out. She looked wild and scary.*

*"I told you to stay in your room!" she shouted as she dragged Macy from the room.*

*Something red on the wall caught Macy's eyes... blood...*

*The room swirled. Everything went black.*

*Then suddenly she was outside. Her mother screaming at her to sleep in the doghouse where she belonged. The rain was coming down hard, big pellets that stung her cheeks and soaked through her pajamas. Her feet were soaked, and a chill cut through her.*

*"Please don't leave me, Mama," Macy cried.*

*But her mother slammed the door shut and Macy heard the lock click.*

*Thunder boomed again, the lightning shattering the dark sky and dancing across the tops of the trees. A noise from the woods made her startle, and she started to cry. Terrified, she ran around the back of the house. The porch and doghouse were too rotten to hide under. Water was pouring through the holes like a river flooding.*

*The house next door had a nice porch. It was covered and safe from the rain. Her bare feet slipped as she slogged through the mud and wove through the bushes. When she reached the porch, she crawled beneath the cover, then sank onto the dry ground. She hugged her knees, cold and shivering.*

Macy jerked herself from the memory. She'd forgotten some of the details of that night. What had happened in her house? She'd blanked out for a minute. Had tidbits of different memories over the years that didn't make sense.

Had there been blood on the wall?

STONE SCANNED THE area surrounding the pawnshop as he pulled into a parking spot. He cut the engine, searching for signs the thief might still be here. But the parking lot was empty, and he didn't see anyone lurking around. The front window had been shattered, and glass had sprayed all over the ground.

Still, he pulled his gun as he climbed from the vehicle and walked up to the door. With each step, he searched the woods beyond. The older concrete building was freestanding and sat on a corner where the road forked. One direction led to mountain cabins popular for vacationers while the other led to camping and hunting grounds. An outfitter store sat catercorner across the way.

The owner, sixty-six-year-old Hazel LeCroy, met him at the door, looking frazzled and angry. Her long wiry gray hair was frizzy with the humidity, her usual outfit of a flannel shirt and jeans rumpled. "Hey, Sheriff," Hazel said with a wave. "Thanks for coming. I can't believe I've been robbed."

"Were you here when the store was broken into?" Stone asked.

Hazel rubbed at the back of her head. "Sure was. In the back. I heard a loud noise, the window shattering, and grabbed my shotgun and came running. But someone jumped me from behind and hit me over the damn head."

Anger at the person who'd hit Hazel surged through Stone. The older woman might be tough as nails and knew how to shoot, but still she was a grandmother.

"Did you see who hit you?"

"No, like I said they jumped me from behind. I

reckon I ought to be glad they didn't shoot me, but they got away with two of my guns."

"We'll get to that," Stone said. "Tell me what happened before the break-in. Have you been busy today? Any customers come in who seemed suspicious?"

"You mean casing the place?" Hazel pulled her frizzy hair back into a ponytail, snapping the rubber band with her thin fingers.

"Yes," Stone said. "Maybe even a couple or a pair working together. Someone who asked about what you had in your case but left without buying anything?"

Hazel shook her head. "Only folks been in were a couple of hunters stocking up on ammo."

"No kids?" Stone asked, holding his breath.

Hazel gestured across the street. "Saw a couple of teens over at the outfitter's store, but they didn't come here."

They could have been watching to see if any customers showed up, left, then parked up the road and sneaked in on foot.

Stone gestured toward the light post where a security camera had been placed. "Let me take a look at the footage."

"Camera don't work," she muttered.

Stone silently cursed. "Call someone and get it fixed. I'll get my forensic kit and look around. If we're dealing with amateurs or teens, maybe they left some prints."

FURIOUS WITH HERSELF for letting the memories get to her, Macy straightened and banished them from her mind. She had a job to do, and she might as well get to it.

Her phone buzzed, and she checked the number. When she saw it was her boss at the Bureau, Special Advisory Director Abraham Holland, she connected. "Hello, Chief."

"How are things going?"

Macy wiped a hand over her face and pulled herself together. "Fine. I'm planning to clean out and put my mother's house on the market ASAP. Hopefully I'll be back at work next week."

"That fast?"

Stone's face flashed in her mind, but that reunion dance last night meant nothing.

No use getting any more involved. Work was her coping mechanism, and she would be leaving soon. "Yes. There's nothing for me here." Nothing but painful reminders of the miserable childhood and the fact that her mother hadn't loved her.

Stone had his own life.

She hung up, yanked her long dark hair into a pony tail, and hurried back outside to her Ford Escape. Now that she had a definite timeline, she opened the trunk and pulled out the giant box of garbage bags she'd bought. She'd probably toss out most everything, but she might donate some items to Goodwill. Although judging from the state of the house and furniture, she doubted much would be salvageable.

Outside, the rain had fizzled out, leaving a cloying humid air. Sweat beaded on her forehead. A sudden feeling that someone was watching her from the shadows of the woods again swept over her, and she surveyed the property.

Brush shifted and crackled. Leaves fluttered to the ground. A deer scampered through the forest.

Another reason she had to leave this place. Old ghosts haunted her, resurrecting her childhood fears and insecurities. Sure, she chased real live monsters on the job, but they were tangible and impersonal. Saving victims helped her forget the fact that she hadn't saved Kate's mother or any other students the day of the infamous school massacre.

Anxious to be finished, she hurried inside to tackle the kitchen. Pushing up her sleeves, she yanked on rubber gloves and started with the pantry. A few canned goods, tuna, peanut butter, all outdated, along with a bag of bug-infested sugar and flour. A box of cereal that was nearly empty, and a canister of rice also full of insects. Old cooking oil and spices that hadn't been used in at least a decade.

Her mother had never been a cook. Obviously, that hadn't changed after Macy left.

The refrigerator came next. The stench nearly knocked her over. She tossed the condiments and the rotting meat into the bag, tied it, then carried it outside to the dumpster.

The next few hours she spent going through the cabinets. None of the rusted pans, cracked dishes or plasticware warranted donating, so she pitched them into the trash. The drawers held junk and old bills that needed paying and her mother's work calendars so she left those for now until she could go through each one.

A set of kitchen knives on the counter made her pause and sweat beaded her neck as a snippet of a memory flashed through her mind. Her mother… a knife in hand…blood trickling down her arm.

Macy stiffened. Had she cut herself?

Jerking back to the present, she noticed one of the knives was missing from the set. She looked around but didn't find it anywhere in the kitchen. Deciding it didn't matter, she left the others on the counter in case she needed a knife for some reason.

The bathroom came next. Nothing salvageable there. Toiletries, a toothbrush, half-empty toothpaste tube, hair spray and cheap makeup. Bottles of painkillers and over-the-counter drugs filled the medicine cabinet, so she raked those into the bag.

Next, she jerked down the faded shower curtain and liner and tossed those. She tackled the den next, piling the magazines and knickknacks into the trash.

Her childhood bedroom came next.

For a moment, she couldn't breathe as she stepped inside the room. But the sight of her track posters ripped and shredded hardened her, and she tore through the room, swiping the few dolls and toys she'd once had from the shelves, then emptying the drawers of high school notebooks she'd used for assignments.

No sentimental attachments. When she'd left home, she'd never looked back.

She cleaned out the closet, filling another bag with the clothing items she'd left behind. Jeans, T-shirts, tennis shoes…nothing was worth keeping or giving away.

Most had been secondhand when she'd gotten them and were so out of style no kid would want them now. Her hand raked over the top shelf where she'd kept the shoebox of photos and ribbons from her track meets, and pictures of her, Kate and Brynn.

A couple of pictures of them were the only things she'd taken with her.

When her room was cleaned out, she started on her mother's. Adrenaline churning, she quickly scooped up her clothing, shoes and the bedding and filled another bag. She didn't pause to reminisce although an image of her mother sprawled in a drug-induced state on the bed taunted her. How many times had she helped her mother to bed?

How many times had Macy locked herself in her room to keep her mother from coming in and taking her wrath out on her?

Pulse pounding, she spent the next hour hauling the smaller pieces of furniture to the dumpster, then grabbed a bottle of water and phoned a service to pick up the sofa, kitchen table and beds.

Covered in dust and grime, and sweating, she sipped her water, but stopping gave her time to think, and she turned to face the basement door.

Her head swam with the sound of her mother's voice. *"Never go down there, Macy." Her mother jerked her arm, shook her and forced her to look into her eyes. "Never. Do you understand me?"*

Macy's heart pounded at the memory. Then the night of the terrible storm and the noises and the screams. The red splattered on the walls…

Her lungs strained for air. She had never been down there.

But she couldn't sell the place without cleaning it out.

Hands shaking, she found the key to the basement door on top of the refrigerator where her mother had kept it, then inserted it into the lock.

Her mother had made the basement off-limits for a reason.

Did she have the courage to find out why?

# *Chapter Two*

Stone finished searching the pawnshop for forensics, but according to Hazel, several people had been in the store over the last twenty-four hours. It was going to be difficult to sort out what was what. He'd taken special care to dust the glass case where the guns had been kept, but most likely the thief had worn gloves. He found a rock outside that had probably been used to smash the window and bagged it.

"A .38 Special was taken," Hazel said. "And a .22."

He jotted down the contact information for the original owners to follow up in case one of them decided they wanted their weapon back and didn't have the money.

"You got someone coming to fix those cameras?"

Hazel nodded. "In the morning. I also called about having the glass window and gun case replaced."

"I'll board up the window for you for tonight and have my deputy do a drive-by this evening." If word leaked the pawnshop was compromised, looters might come. The last thing he needed was more guns on the street.

MACY'S PULSE CLAMORED as she opened the door to the basement. The steps were pitch-black, the air musty, dust coating the stair rail. She reached for an overhead light and flicked it, but nothing happened.

Suffocating as the darkness engulfed her, she flipped the switch again, but the light was burned out. Pulling her phone from her pocket, she aimed the flashlight at the stairs. Cobwebs dangled from the rail and ceiling, and she pushed them away with her gloved hands and tiptoed down the steps. The boards creaked and moaned, buckling beneath her feet as if they might give way any second.

Her pulse jumped with every step she took, dread curling in her belly. One step, two, three, slowly she descended, aiming the light around the concrete floor and dingy walls. Shadows seemed to jump out of nowhere, the sound of water pinging onto the floor and trickling down the wall echoing in the tense silence.

Her mother's voice taunted her again. *Never go down there, Macy. Never.*

Ignoring the voice, she moved on, determined to break this hold her mother had on her. She was no longer a child. Her mother couldn't hurt her anymore. She'd see what was down here once and for all, quiet her imagination from the horrors of what she'd feared, and then her nightmares would cease.

A few boxes sat in one corner, along with a broken rocking chair and an ancient armoire. Shelves on one wall held cleaning chemicals her mother had used when she worked as a housekeeper. The sound of the water pinged, a stench assaulting her. She aimed her flashlight around the room and spotted the source. The far wall. The ceiling was leaking, water trickling down the wall and onto the floor. The rain or one of the toilets?

Mold grew along the baseboard and up the wall fanning out in a spiderweb-like pattern. The acrid odor grew stronger as she walked toward the source; the walls were pocked with holes where the drywall had literally rotted away.

Her heart hammered as she shone the light along the space. What had her mother not wanted her to see down here?

The armoire. Holding her breath, she crossed the room to it, then reached for the door. Her fingers clasped the metal latch, and she pulled it open, bracing herself.

But her breath whooshed out when she realized it was empty.

Stumbling sideways to take a breath, she bumped the damp wall, then felt the drywall give way in one section. Hurling herself away from it, she gasped in horror.

Bones protruded through the opening, the skeleton of a hand curled as if clawing to escape.

STONE'S PHONE BUZZED just as he was leaving the pawnshop. A quick check of the number, and he saw it was Macy.

He quickly connected and said hello.

"Stone..." Her voice cracked. "Y-you need to come out here."

Her voice was raw, pained. Something was wrong. "Come where?"

"My mother's old house," she said, her voice shaky. "I f-found a body in the basement."

Stone stood, tension coiling inside him. He heard the fear in her voice, could see her big brown eyes filled with terror. "I'll be right there."

MACY STAGGERED BACKWARD, her phone nearly slipping through her fingers. Unable to drag her gaze away from the skeletal hand, she visually scanned the hole and noticed a larger hole above it.

Bile rose to her throat as she spotted the skull, eyes mere hollow sockets staring back at her.

Her first instinct was to start ripping away the rest of the wall and expose the body inside, but her detective instincts kicked in, and she reminded herself not to touch anything.

Mental images of what might have happened here flooded her.

Had her mother known the body was down here? Had she found it?

Or had she put it in the wall?

Trembling at the thought that her mother might be a killer, she covered her mouth with her hand, then turned, crossed to the stairs and climbed them. The squeaky steps sounded even more eerie now, her erratic breathing louder. She fought images of her mother in one of her out-of-control states unleashing her rage in such a violent manner. Panic-stricken when she realized what she'd done. Stuffing the body in the wall, then covering it with new drywall and leaving it to decompose while she lived upstairs and went on about her life. While her own child slept in a bedroom above the hellhole where she'd disposed of a body.

She pushed through the door to the hall, breathing out raggedly, desperate to blot the images from her mind. But they bombarded her, tearing at her control, and she stumbled toward the living room, then opened the front door and stepped outside. The rain had ceased, the scent of damp grass lingering, rainwater still dripping from the gutters, a reminder of the leak in the basement.

Dizzy, she gripped the porch rail, leaned over and dragged in several deep breaths, a chill invading her that had nothing to do with the rain. She rocked back and forth, her body shaking, as she looked at the gloomy sky. Seconds bled into minutes, tension thrumming through her.

The sound of a siren shattered the silence, and relief poured through her as the sheriff's SUV careened into the driveway. She lifted her chin and pulled herself together. She was an FBI agent. This wasn't the first body she'd seen.

Except none had been in her own house. None had been personal.

Stone cut the siren and lights, then stepped from his vehicle and strode toward her. A faint hint of the moon peeked through the rain clouds, illuminating his chiseled face and his strong square jaw.

His boots pounded the wooden steps as he climbed them, then he stopped in front of her, hazel eyes narrowed and full of concern. "Macy?"

The gruff timbre of his tone was her undoing. He reached for her arms, stroked them, forcing her to look at him. The worry reflected in his eyes shattered her resistance.

Choking out his name, she leaned into him, her body trembling as he wrapped his arms around her.

STONE RUBBED MACY'S BACK, gently soothing her. She was a tough agent, but whatever had happened had really shaken her.

Which meant it was bad.

He held her until her trembling slowly subsided, and she pulled away from him.

"I'm sorry about that," she murmured.

"No problem. Talk to me," he said. "What happened?"

She brushed her damp eyes with the back of her hand, then leaned against the railing and gestured toward the dumpster. Though her dark hair was damp from rain, and her clothes dusty, she still was beautiful. "I was cleaning out the house, tossing most everything."

"To get the house ready to sell?"

She nodded. "I got most of the bedrooms and kitchen done. Then I…decided to check the basement." Her voice wavered. "It was dark, and the light was burned out, but I heard water dripping and wanted to see what it was."

"Go on."

She released a labored breath. "I used my phone flashlight and saw water leaking from the ceiling.

I went closer and noticed the wall was rotten and there was a big hole in it. And then I saw it."

"The body?"

Macy nodded again, her gaze haunted. "It's inside the wall."

Stone swallowed hard. If the body was in the wall, that meant it probably wasn't fresh. That someone put it there. Not an accident or a loner hiding out. "A man or woman?"

"I don't know. It's decomposed. Just bones."

"So it's been there for a while," Stone said.

"It looks that way. All I could see was the hand and the skull where the plaster was rotted through." Macy rubbed her arms with her hands. "We need a recovery team and the medical examiner."

"And a forensics team," Stone said. "I'll make the call."

Macy turned to look out at the woods as he phoned the medical examiner and the CSI team. Her faraway look made him wonder what was going on in her head.

"I'm going to take a look myself," Stone said when he hung up.

"I'll show you."

"No need for you to go back inside, Macy. I can handle it. Wait here for the crime team and ME."

She murmured okay, then he went to his SUV, grabbed gloves, boot covers and a flashlight, and carried them back to the porch.

"The door to the basement is in the hall," Macy said.

He geared up before entering the house. He'd

never been inside Macy's, and she hadn't been back for years. It showed in the dust, the stuffy odor and the weathered furniture. She said she'd cleaned out things, and that showed, too. Except for a tattered orange vinyl sofa and plaid armchair, the living room looked bare. He crossed to the hall, flicked on his flashlight and started down the steps. The stairs gave way in places, hinting at rot, and he gripped the stair rail to steady his footing. The sound of water dripping and pinging off the floor drew his attention toward the far corner.

The acrid odor of mildew and old body decomp hit him, and he covered his mouth with his handkerchief as he reached the landing. Shining his flashlight across the space, he spotted an antique armoire, then the damp wall where plaster had cracked and rot had created gaping holes.

The stench grew stronger as he walked toward the corner, and he aimed his flashlight onto the wall. The grisly sight of the skeletal remains poking through the opening made him halt in his tracks. He couldn't imagine how shocked Macy had felt.

This place had been her home.

Now it was a crime scene.

# *Chapter Three*

Macy's mind raced as various scenarios played through her head. Perhaps she was wrong about her mother's involvement with that body.

Although she couldn't shake the memory of that awful stormy night. Her mother had been in one of her moods and had screamed at her, but she'd done that before.

Hadn't she? Or had that been the first time?

Her memory of the years before that were muddy. For some reason that one evening seemed to be a pivotal moment.

She'd been terrified and alone. But Kate's mother had found her outside and taken her in, and then she and Kate had become best friends.

Her mother had been distant after that.

Had something happened that night? Had her mother known the body was in the wall?

It was possible that someone had put it there before they moved in. That her mother hadn't known. Or that she'd found it and that had triggered her to have a breakdown.

*Or maybe you're grasping. Maybe she killed*

*whoever it was and hid him in the wall so no one would find him. Or discover what she'd done.*

She closed her eyes, trying to sort through the events of that night again. But the sound of an engine cut through the silence, and she jerked her eyes open to see a van roll into her drive. On the heels of it came a black sedan that she assumed belonged to the medical examiner's office.

The crime investigators slid from the van, the county logo for the crime lab emblazoned on their shirts, then gathered their kits and walked toward her. A young woman with ebony skin and black hair pulled into a bun followed from the sedan, her medical bag in hand.

Macy shut off her emotions and launched into agent mode.

The CSI team paused at the top of the stairs, and the woman followed. Macy introduced herself and flashed her credentials.

"Dr. Latoya Anderson, ME." She extended her hand, and Macy shook it.

The crime investigators introduced themselves as Wesley Moore and Kat Parker. And Stone reappeared, looking grim faced.

Macy explained about finding the corpse. "It's decomposed, just the skeletal remains, indicating it's been there for some time. I haven't been home in years. I was cleaning out things to put the house on the market." Now that plan would have to be postponed. Her childhood home was literally the scene of a possible homicide. "I'm afraid I touched almost everything upstairs when I was going through things."

"Did you see anything that pointed to murder?" Stone interjected.

Macy pinched the bridge of her nose, thinking. "Not that I recall. Mostly it was canned food, trash, magazines, some clothing and old toiletries. But I can hold off on having the dumpster picked up in case we need to search it."

"Probably a good idea," Stone agreed. "You never know if there's a clue in something that seems innocuous."

"True." She turned to the crime team. "My prints are on file for elimination purposes. But concentrate on processing the basement." She addressed the medical examiner. "We need to be careful excavating the body."

"Do you have any idea who the victim is?" Dr. Anderson asked.

Macy shook her head. "No, nor do I know how long it's been there or how it got there. Identifying the remains will be a start."

"I'll call a forensic anthropologist to assist with the autopsy," Dr. Anderson said. "But it may take a few days before we can get an ID."

Macy racked her brain for some memory of a man or woman visiting, one her mother had had an altercation with. She struggled for a plausible reason, one that didn't involve her mother being a murderer.

Even if she had killed someone, it could have been self-defense. What if someone had broken in and threatened her? Pulled a gun? She could have tried to protect herself, and even Macy, and things got out of hand.

She closed her eyes again, struggling to tap into her memory banks. But her early years were so fuzzy that her life was defined by that rainy night when her mother had thrown her outside in a crazed rage. There had been more episodes after that that she recalled. She'd never understood what triggered them.

Stone's expression was stark, his voice dragging her from the troubling scenarios playing through her mind.

"Your turn to take a look, Doc," Stone said. "I'll warn you, it's pretty gruesome."

"Gruesome is my day job," Dr. Anderson said wryly. "And you two, call me Latoya."

"I'm Macy, then."

"And Stone," he said. "You want me to walk you down?"

"No, I've got it," Latoya said. "I'm sure you and Macy need to discuss the situation."

Macy tensed, and the ME excused herself and headed down the stairs. Stone rubbed her arm. "You okay?"

Macy choked back a nervous laugh. Was she okay? No, hell no. How could she be okay when she'd just found a body in the wall of her mother's house?

When she might have been sleeping in her room upstairs when the person had been killed and enclosed there?

STONE WATCHED AS the CSI investigators searched and processed the basement and house. He had never been to Macy's in high school. It was definitely not the hangout house. But he'd heard rumors that her mother was unstable. Except for Kate and Brynn, he didn't know if Macy had any other friends.

Although she excelled at track, she hadn't joined in on the after-school sports teams get-togethers. He'd never seen her at a school dance or prom and had been surprised when he heard she'd married Trey Cushing. He'd never liked the jerk, thought he was a bully, although at one time he supposed the girls found him charming.

But he'd heard the disrespectful way Trey talked about girls and didn't like it.

Dr. Anderson confirmed that the victim was a male. It took hours for the crime team to process the basement and remove the skeletal remains. The recovery team had to be careful not to damage the bones or destroy any forensics that might have been left behind so the ME could determine cause and general time of death.

"We found hair and fibers of clothing that are partially decayed, but we might be able to get something from them," one of the investigators told Macy. "We also found traces of blood in the wall and on the clothing. We'll send it all to the lab."

Macy showed them the bags of clothing she'd collected from her mother's room, and one of the CSIs went through it, searching for blood or hair fibers, although after so many years, it would be difficult to determine their origin or how long they'd been there.

Dawn was just streaking the sky when they finally finished. Yellow crime scene tape encircled the house with the warning not to enter.

Macy looked pale and shell-shocked, her dark hair a tangled mess where it had escaped her pony tail.

"You can't stay here," Stone said.

"I wasn't planning to," Macy said with a shiver. "I have a room at the inn in town."

"Let me drive you," Stone offered.

"Thanks, but I need my car to get around town." As anxious as she was to get out of Briar Ridge, she couldn't leave until she knew the truth about what had happened here.

EXHAUSTION MINGLED WITH the shock of the night as Macy parked at the Rosebud Inn. In spite of the vibrant red and orange streaking the morning sky, dread curled in her belly as questions needled her.

Dammit. Her mother might hold the answers… which meant she had to visit her. That had not been on the agenda. But she had no choice now.

Her chest clenched as she grabbed her bag and entered the Victorian house that the owner, Celeste, had recently renovated. When Kate pushed to build the new school, it sparked a wave of store owners and businesses that had fallen in disrepair the last fifteen years to make some much-needed updates.

Celeste had added a rose garden, gazebo by the pond and fresh paint on the exterior. She'd also remodeled the rooms inside with themes, hoping to draw tourists back to the area. The mountain ridges rose in the background, sunlight shimmering off the peaks, promising a sunny day compared to the gray storm clouds yesterday.

For a short few days, Briar Ridge had felt a sense of hope in the aftermath of a long storm. The new school was opening. A memorial had been created to honor the fallen students and Kate's mother, who'd died protecting her pupils. Former classmates and residents had started to build relationships and trust again. Tourists were starting to return, renting cabins, camping, hiking and enjoying the outdoor activities the scenic mountains offered.

But that sense of peace and trust was about to end. Soon everyone in town would know about her discovery. Once again, her family would feed the gossip train with whispers and accusations. Tears blurred Macy's eyes as she slipped inside past the front desk. The scent of coffee, pancakes and bacon wafted to her from the kitchen where Celeste was preparing breakfast for the guests.

Her stomach roiled. She was too exhausted to eat. Right now she needed sleep and quiet before she had to face the media frenzy that would start when the news leaked.

Gretta Wright, one of her classmates who'd run a gossip rag in high school, had now joined the professional journalism ranks and was a local newscaster. Like a raptor stalking its prey, she'd lunge on the story—and Macy's possible involvement. She'd already had a field day with the fact that Macy had arrested her ex for giving Ned Hodgkins the gun he'd used to slaughter their classmates.

Before the story broke, though, Macy wanted to find the answers. As soon as she got some rest, she'd visit her mother and make her talk.

AS STONE DROVE toward his cabin on the creek, he phoned his deputy to handle the routine work in the office so he could go home and grab some z's. It would take time for the lab to process the blood and forensics, look for a DNA match. Meanwhile, he'd refuel.

Although Macy's pained face taunted him. She'd looked so forlorn that he'd wanted to comfort her, but he reminded himself to remain professional. She'd never intended to stay in Briar Ridge. Had told him from the start that she'd be leaving town after the class reunion and resuming her own life.

No sense in getting too close to her when he knew that. He'd been down that road before, thank you very much. His high school girlfriend Joanna had bolted after graduation, too. Said she didn't want small-town life. She wanted to see the world. Had headed to New York City, and he'd never heard from her again.

Macy would do the same.

But now they had a crime to solve. There was no way she could sell that house until they did.

The road from Macy's toward his cabin was devoid of traffic, but when he turned onto the street outside town he spotted his brother staggering down the road, walking along the shoulder in the direction of his apartment. Worry and anger slammed into him, and he slowly eased up beside him. Mickey stumbled and nearly fell, flailing to keep from falling into the ditch.

Stone gritted his teeth, then pulled over, gravel spewing as he skidded to a stop. He shoved open the door of his squad car, shaking his head as Mickey wove back and forth. Fearing he'd slip or get hit by a car, he jogged to him.

Mickey's eyes were glassy and half-closed as he slowly turned him to face Stone. "What the hell, Mickey?"

His brother grunted, wobbling sideways. "What are you doing here?"

"I was on my way home from a case I worked last night," Stone said, the stench of booze hitting him in the face. "You're drunk, little brother. Come on, I'll drive you home."

Mickey yanked his arm away. "Leave me alone. I didn't ask you to come."

"No, you didn't. But I'm taking you home anyway." He'd already lost enough people in his life. Mickey pulled back and stumbled toward the embankment, and Stone grabbed him just in time to keep him from falling into the rocks. His brother cursed as Stone hauled him to his squad car, opened the door and helped him inside. Before Stone could make it to the driver's seat, Mickey had passed out cold.

Worry knotted his gut, the guilt overwhelming him. He'd promised his father he'd watch out for Mickey. But somehow he'd already let him down.

# *Chapter Four*

Macy slept fitfully for three hours, then jerked awake and stared at the cracks in the ceiling. Ever since she was a child, night had been her enemy. The dark filled her with dread, the uncertainty of her mother's moods plaguing her with anxiety.

Track had become her stress release and she'd been jogging ever since. As soon as she climbed from bed, she dressed in running clothes and shoes and hit the sidewalk outside.

She hadn't seen her mother in years. Today she not only had to face her, but she had to ask her about a dead man.

The midday sun beamed down on her, the humid air making her hair stick to the back of her neck as she jogged into the heart of town. Her ponytail bobbed up and down, her heart racing as she picked up her pace. The town square held a park and walking trail where families and mothers were out strolling with their children, and kids played at the park in the center.

She passed Pearl's Dine & Pie which was packed with the lunch crowd, then Joy's Fabrics & Crafts.

As she reached the Cut & Dye she couldn't help but think about Cassidy Fulton, who worked there. Cassidy was another former student, one who'd actually slept with Ned before the shooting and had his baby. She'd kept that secret for years, but it had come out recently.

The place offered full salon services, including hairstyling, highlights, mani-pedis, massages and waxing. The rumor mill usually started there, spreading quickly from one hairdryer to the next. She'd heard Cassidy was moving. The publicity over the fact that Ned Hodgkins had fathered Cassidy's son, and her son had been arrested for trying to hurt Kate, was probably more than she could take.

The tension in Macy's shoulders eased with every mile, and her courage returned. She was a trained FBI agent, had gotten out of a terrible marriage and taken down notorious criminals. She could confront her own mother without falling apart.

With last night on her mind, as she passed the sheriff's office, she decided to check with Stone to see if he'd heard from the lab.

Wiping perspiration from her forehead, she entered the office and greeted the receptionist, Hattie Mae Perkins. While working with Stone the last couple of weeks, she'd learned that Hattie was new on the job but had lived in Briar Ridge all her life. She also liked to bake and kept the break room furnished with cookies and cakes.

"Is Sheriff Lawson in?"

"Not yet. He had a late night."

She knew all about that. Soon everyone else in Briar Ridge would. "Thanks. I'll give him a call."

She ducked outside and jogged back toward the inn, but as she turned the corner past the bookstore, the hair on the back of her neck prickled. She scanned the street, the sense that someone was watching her hitting her full force.

Then she saw a group of ladies hovering, whispering, watching her. Gretta Wright stood talking to them. She looked over at Macy and made eye contact, a twinkle in her eyes as if they were talking about her.

Had someone already leaked news about the murder?

STONE SILENTLY CURSED as he stared at his little brother, who was still passed out on the couch where he'd left him early this morning. A few hours of sleep for him, but now he was back and his brother looked nowhere near ready to get up and work.

He had no idea what was going on with Mickey. For a while after the shooting, he'd been depressed and had a chip on his shoulder.

But school for the visually impaired had helped him adjust and taught him coping skills, and then he'd turned his interest in video games and music into a job by working for an online company.

He nudged him with his knee. "Come on, Mickey. I brought you a breakfast sandwich. I'll make coffee and we can talk."

Mickey groaned, then rolled to his back and pressed his hand over his eyes. "Go away. I'm tired."

"You're hungover," Stone growled. "What about work today?"

"I'll get to it." He rolled to his side and tugged the pillow over his head. "Don't you need to be out playing the hero somewhere?"

"I'm no hero," Stone said, his voice laced with self-disgust. Why did his brother sound bitter toward him? "Tell me what's going on," he said, softening his tone. "I can't help you if I don't know."

"I don't need your help," Mickey snarled.

Stone's cell phone buzzed. Macy.

"I gotta go. Get up, clean yourself up and eat something, Mickey. And call me when you do."

"Yeah, yeah, yeah," Mickey muttered.

Stone clenched his phone and answered as he stepped outside his brother's apartment.

"It's Macy," she said a little breathlessly as if she was running. "Have you heard anything from the ME or lab yet?"

"No, hopefully sometime later today, but that may be pushing it."

The sound of a car honking echoed in the background. "I'm going to talk to my mother," Macy said.

Stone slid into his squad car. "I'll go with you."

A tense second passed. "That's not necessary, Stone. I can handle it."

He heaved a breath. "Macy, you know how this works. It's a homicide investigation and you have a conflict of interest."

"Don't you trust me?" Macy said, anger lacing her voice.

"It's not about trust," he said. "It's about protocol. You know we have to follow the rules and the clues, no matter where they lead us."

Even if it meant he had to arrest her mother.

MACY KNEW STONE was just doing his job. But confiding her family secrets was something she thought she'd never do. Some things needed to stay buried.

Maybe that's what her mother had decided about the body…

But now that it had been exposed, Macy couldn't ignore it or cover it up.

"I'm jogging," Macy said. "Give me thirty minutes for a shower and some coffee."

"Okay. I'll pick you up in a little bit."

She agreed and hung up, looking over her shoulder and all around her as she rushed into the inn. She'd half expected Gretta to follow her or show up any minute. But she breathed out in relief when she didn't see her.

Celeste still had hot coffee and pastries on the buffet in the dining room, so she grabbed a cup of coffee and a Danish and carried it to her room—the Orchid Room. Painted a soft, soothing lilac, the room felt like a retreat from the ugliness of the outside world. She ate, then stripped her running clothes and climbed into the shower. The hot water helped soothe her aching body, and she closed her eyes and scrubbed her hair, but the grisly image from the night before taunted her.

Once again, her mother had found a way to sabotage her life. Anger was the only way she'd survived before, so she latched on to it. She dried her hair, then pulled it back into a ponytail and dressed in a blue T-shirt and jeans. No need to dress the part of the FBI. That would only intimidate her mother and trigger a defensive reaction.

Grabbing her shoulder purse, she stowed her phone and weapon inside, then left the room, locked it and hurried down the steps to the front door. By the time she stepped outside, Stone was parking. She jogged over to his squad car and slipped into the passenger side.

"We're going to Bear Mountain Gardens," Macy said.

Stone's dark eyes flashed with emotions she couldn't quite define. "You ready for this?"

No. Hell no. "Just drive," she said quietly.

He nodded, stepped on the gas and pulled from the parking lot. Macy turned and looked out the window at the passing scenery as he wove through town.

The last time she'd seen her mother, they'd screamed at each other. Her mother had been in one of her manic states, ranting and throwing things and blaming Macy for all her problems.

Sometimes she thought her mother had wished she'd never been born.

TENSION RADIATED IN the silence as Stone drove through the secure gates and parked in the circular drive in front of the main entrance to Bear Mountain Gardens.

Hoping she'd open up on her own, he'd decided not to push Macy to talk.

The assisted living facility was set on ten acres

and divided into sections based on the senior's needs. One area served the assisted living, another focused on housing for memory care, and another doubled as a halfway house type situation for those undergoing counseling for mental disorders and addiction. Staff included nurses, doctors, certified nursing assistants, counselors, and occupational therapists. Medications were monitored by the staff.

Social activities were organized for residents in a community center, and the landscape outside provided walking trails and a flower and vegetable garden that the residents themselves tended to.

Macy shifted as he parked, her breath heavy with dread.

"I don't know what happened between you two, but I sense it wasn't pleasant," he said gently.

Macy angled her head to look at him, her eyes swimming in pain. "My mother suffers from bipolar disorder. She's manic one minute and depressive the next. When she took her meds, she was easier to handle. When she didn't, which was more often than she did, she got ugly." She reached for the door handle and opened the door. "That's why she's here. To monitor her meds and keep her stable."

Stone swallowed against the emotions the empty hollowness in her tone stirred. "She hurt you?"

Macy gave a small shrug but ignored the question, then got out and slammed the car door.

Her withdrawal made his chest clench. The rumors he'd heard at school and in town obviously had merit.

Just what had her mother done to her behind closed doors?

# *Chapter Five*

The only time Macy had been to Bear Mountain Gardens was when her mother was admitted. She'd never told anyone about that day. Instead, she'd locked the pain in the darkest corners of her mind out of reach and hopefully forgotten.

But now the memory tumbled through the door and slammed into her with the crushing weight of a boulder.

*"You can't leave me here, Macy!" her mother screamed. "I'm your mother."*

*Her mother's doctor, a kind middle-aged woman named Dr. Garrett, had intervened. "We talked about this, Lynn," the doctor said gently. "You agreed to stay here and undergo therapy so you could get better."*

*"It's her fault I'm like this," her mother cried. "It's Macy's fault."*

*"Macy did not make this decision," Dr. Garrett said firmly. "The court ordered you to undergo treatment in a monitored facility."*

*"I didn't do what she said I did!" her mother screeched.*

*Macy instinctively rubbed a finger over the scar on the back of her neck, the one her mother had given her when she'd knocked her against the corner of the table.*

*"Give the program a try," Dr. Garrett said. "You have a chemical imbalance that affects your moods. The medication will stabilize those moods and help you live a more productive life." The psychiatrist patted her mother's back. "I'll be with you every step of the way."*

*But her mother wasn't responding to the doctor's calm tone or assurances. She looked wild-eyed and crazed, and suddenly shoved the doctor away from her with such force that Dr. Garrett stumbled backward and grabbed the wall for support. Then she ran for the door.*

*Dr. Garrett recovered quickly and motioned to the male nurse at the door, who caught her mother before she could escape the room. She swung her fists at the man, beating him in the chest as she screamed and kicked.*

*Dr. Garrett gave Macy a sympathetic look, removed a hypodermic from her pocket, then calmly walked over and gave Macy's mother the injection.*

*Her mother turned a venomous look toward Macy.*

*"What did I do to you to make you lock me in here?"*

Pain nearly choked Macy at the accusation. She'd done lots of things to Macy, but Macy had never told. She'd tried to pretend that they had a normal life.

But nothing in her household had been normal.

She pulled herself from the past. Kate and her mother had known. They'd seen her erratic behavior themselves.

After Macy left town, her mother had gotten worse. She'd received numerous calls from the police where she'd been found drugged and on a rampage.

Not in Briar Ridge, but always close to wherever Macy was living. She'd been stalking her. And then the attack…

A shudder coursed up her spine.

Stone remained a quiet force by her side, yet humiliation washed over her at the idea of airing her family's dirty secrets in front of him.

Pulling her credentials, she identified herself to the nurse's assistant at the front desk and explained she needed to see her mother.

The young redhead called Dr. Garrett and informed her of their arrival. The psychiatrist had sent her reports on her mother's condition the past year after she'd been admitted. Before that, Macy had rarely visited since she left town and then only for holidays or when her mother's doctor called because she'd had an episode. Some days were good. Others she slipped. Dr. Garrett believed that with the right kind of therapy they'd uncover the source of what had triggered her mother's condition to decline and to learn the source of her psychotic break.

Now Macy might have a clue to help fill in the gaps.

STONE FELT FOR MACY, but his job was to uncover the truth about a crime and protect the citizens of Briar Ridge, and he intended to do it.

Even if it meant asking Macy tough questions or keeping her out of the loop.

When Dr. Garrett arrived, Macy introduced them and asked to speak in private.

"Of course." The plump woman led them down a carpeted hallway past several offices, then to her own. Her diplomas and awards hung in frames on the plain beige wall, documenting her degree, residency, fellowships and experience. Yellow gerbera daisies filled a vase on the desk, which was neat and organized.

She offered them coffee, and they both accepted. Macy looked eager for it, or maybe she just wanted something to do with her fidgety hands. Then they claimed chairs in a seating area in the corner of the room, which looked cozy and was obviously meant to make her patients feel at ease.

"What's this about, Macy?" Dr. Garrett asked.

Stone appreciated her direct approach.

"I came home to clean out my mother's house and put it on the market, but I found something very disturbing last night. I need to ask my mother about it," Macy began.

She inhaled sharply, then gestured to Stone. He silently thanked her for letting him take the lead. Maybe she did recognize that she couldn't be objective in this situation.

The doctor narrowed her eyes. "I'm guessing from the fact that the sheriff is with you that this is not just a social visit."

Macy shook her head and Stone cleared his throat.

"Dr. Garrett, last night Macy—Agent Stark—found a dead person's remains in the wall in the basement of her mother's house."

Dr. Garrett's eyes widened in shock, and she glanced back and forth between them. "Oh, my word."

"At this point, we haven't identified the man," Stone explained. "But judging from decomp, we believe the bones have been there for some time."

Macy's face paled. "The state of decomp suggests the body was there when my mother still lived at home," Macy said. "That means we have to question her."

Dr. Garrett's forehead wrinkled as she processed the statement. "Are you suggesting that someone was murdered in the house?"

Stone gave her a grim look. "It's possible. It's also possible that the person was killed elsewhere and stored in the wall afterward, but if Mrs. Stark was living at the house at the time, that would have been difficult to do without her knowledge."

"But her mental state..." The doctor cut herself off. "With HIPAA laws, I can't discuss Lynn's medical history in front of anyone except Macy, her legal guardian. Not unless I have permission. I also can't allow you to question her without my presence."

Stone expected HIPAA to complicate the situation. And for the doctor to insist on being present.

Macy sighed heavily. "I give my permission for you to discuss her condition in front of Sheriff Lawson. No one else but him. We have to find out what happened in that house."

Macy's pained tone tore at Stone, but she was FBI. She knew the drill. And she obviously wanted answers.

Dr. Garrett studied them both for a long minute. "All right. But if Lynn does know about this body, then it could have been the trigger for her psychotic break, so we have to tread carefully. That means you let me lead the discussion. If I sense she's getting too agitated, or that she's repressed memories of a murder, then we stop, and I'll try therapeutic techniques to help her tap into her memories slowly. The last thing we need is to cause more damage to her psyche." She drummed her fingers on her suit pant leg. "There's also the possibility of TMR."

"What is that?" Stone asked.

"Traumatic memory recovery, although there have been instances during that kind of treatment where patients recalled false memories or events. With bipolar disorder and schizophrenic tendencies, that's a possibility."

She made it sound bleak, Stone thought.

But they had to get answers.

MACY WRESTLED TO control her emotions. Stone had no idea how much it cost her to give him access to her mother's condition. That was opening a closed door to the secrets in her life.

Her face heated at the thought. But she had joined the Bureau to see that justice was served, and she couldn't move forward without closing this chapter in her past.

She and Stone followed Dr. Garrett through the building. She chatted about the facility as they went. One section was designated for patients with medium care, meaning they required checkups to monitor medicine and make sure they made their therapy sessions, versus another unit that was highly secured to keep dangerous, potentially violent patients under lock and key.

Her mother had initially been sequestered to that unit but through cooperative behavior had eventually been moved to the less guarded section, offering her more freedom during the days to roam the gardens and participate in the activities meant to help patients heal and blend into society.

The doctor's monologue saved Macy from talking. Her stomach was churning at the thought of facing her mother again. As many sinister criminals as she'd faced the past few years, none of them turned her into the terrified, quivering little child who had borne the brunt of her mother's rages.

After winding past the solarium and community room, they stepped through French doors that led to the garden area where residents were pruning the plants and tending to the colorful flowers. Several patients/residents were pulling weeds and picking the vegetables that had ripened, filling baskets that would go to the kitchen for dinner preparation.

Macy did not see her mother anywhere.

Dr. Garrett's brow furrowed, and she approached one of the nursing assistants and spoke in a hushed tone. When she turned to Macy, her pulse jumped.

"The nurse said your mother refused to come to the garden today," Dr. Garrett said. "Let's check her suite. She could have overslept."

The nerves in Macy's stomach clawed at her.

Dr. Garrett led them back inside, then down another hallway to her mother's suite. Due to her dangerous nature, she hadn't yet earned a kitchenette, but she had a private room and bath and a window that offered a view of the majestic mountains beyond. It was a little pricey but with insurance and her savings, she managed to make it work, although sometimes her money was tight. Selling her mother's house would definitely help with the budget.

Dr. Garrett knocked and when no answer came, used a key to unlock the door. The moment they opened the door, Macy had a bad feeling.

They checked the bedroom and adjoining bathroom, and no one was inside. But things were scattered all across the room, the window was open and the screen had been slashed.

STONE EXAMINED THE window frame and torn screen, then gave the doctor a questioning look. "It looks like Mrs. Stark cut the screen and climbed out the window. Was there some reason she didn't just go out the door?"

The psychiatrist dug her hands into the pocket of her white coat. "She has seemed agitated this week so we suspected she might be ditching her meds. When she stops them abruptly, she becomes paranoid and experiences delusions."

Macy's quickly drawn breath echoed in the air. "Did you think she was dangerous to herself or the other patients?"

The doctor shrugged. "She was erratic. Yesterday she said someone was watching her. She got into it with another resident and when a guard tried to break it up, she tried to stab him with a fork."

Stone didn't like the picture the doctor was painting. Macy's expression remained neutral, a sign she wasn't surprised at the news. Which told him more than if she'd said something.

"When was the last time anyone saw her?" Stone asked.

Dr. Garrett rubbed her temple. "I'll check with her nurse and get an exact time for you."

"We need to search the entire facility and grounds," Stone said. "If she left on foot, she can't have gotten very far."

Macy squared her shoulders. "Find out if any staff member or visitor's car is missing, too."

The doctor pulled her phone and called security. "We have a missing patient. Lynn Stark. Start a thorough search and put the facility on lockdown. Also, make sure everyone's vehicle is accounted for in case she stole a car and drove away."

"I'd like to see security cams," Stone told her as she hung up.

"Let's split up, then," Macy said. "I have a few more questions for the doctor."

Dr. Garrett called a CNA to show Stone to the central security room, and he left Macy with the psychiatrist.

Although doubts crept in. Had Macy simply wanted to manage their time, or did she want to talk to the doctor alone because she was hiding something?

MACY'S MIND RACED. Where the hell was her mother?

"I'm sorry this happened," Dr. Garrett said, worry knitting her forehead. "I promise we'll do everything possible to find her. We pride ourselves on our residents' safety and well-being."

Macy understood the doctor was concerned about liability issues, but she was more worried about what her mother might do while off her meds. The timing of her disappearance was also disturbing.

"Dr. Garrett, during my mother's therapy sessions, did she mention anything about a body in the wall at our house?"

A tense second passed. "You know I can't violate patient-doctor confidentiality."

Macy gritted her teeth. "I understand, but Sheriff Lawson and I are conducting a homicide investigation. If you have information that pertains to that, you have to talk to me."

The doctor's expression gave nothing away. "We've just barely begun to scratch the surface of the inner workings of her mind," she said. "But I can honestly tell you that she has not mentioned a murder or a body in the house."

Macy sensed the doctor was weighing her words carefully. "Do you know what caused her to have a psychotic break?"

"Not specifically." Dr. Garrett folded her arms. "Oftentimes, a traumatic event in childhood triggers a break later in adults. The patient may or may not recall the event. So far, she's been resistant to hypnosis, which might help."

Macy swallowed hard. "I don't know anything about her childhood," she said. "She refused to talk about her parents or my father. But I remember one night when I was five, she flew into a rage and threw me outside. Now I found this body, it makes me wonder if something happened that night to trigger her episode." Macy shifted. "If she was attacked and killed this man in self-defense or murdered him, could that have been the trigger for her break?"

"A traumatic event like an attack could incite a break, yes." The doctor gave her a sympathetic look. "I understand that growing up with a mentally ill mother can scar a child. Perhaps you need to seek counseling yourself to deal with your own trauma."

Macy bit down on her lip. "It's not about me right now. Has Mother talked about running away?"

Dr. Garrett shrugged. "All of my patients talk about running away at some point. They feel trapped and liken being here to prison. Although as you can see, the accommodations and activities are designed to treat the patient physically, emotionally and mentally. But I will go back and study my notes to see if she referenced a specific place she'd go when she left here."

She might come after her, Macy thought. Or go home.

She turned to study the room. "I'd like to look through her things. Maybe there's something here that will explain the reason she left."

The doctor agreed, then left to check with security and see if they'd found her on the premises. Macy walked over to the small desk in the corner of the room. Above it hung several pages of sketches, all black-and-whites of monsters, all disturbing.

Were those monsters representative of someone in particular?

# *Chapter Six*

Stone spent the next hour studying camera footage with the lead security officer. Dr. Garrett texted saying Mrs. Stark had been in her room around eight for breakfast, although the CNA stated that she was agitated and refused to eat. She left Lynn inside her room, pacing and ranting that someone had tried to break in the night before. That was the last time anyone had seen her.

"Narrow in on the evening and night," Stone told the security officer. "Let's verify that no one actually tried to break into her room."

The officer rolled the footage, and Stone scrutinized the area outside Mrs. Stark's room and the window. Minute after minute passed, and all was quiet and still. They continued to watch through the night hours until morning, but he didn't see anyone lurking outside the window or tampering with the screen.

"Many of the patients here are delusional and paranoid," the officer said. "We've had them get hold of phones and call 911 from their rooms claiming we're trying to kill them."

Stone grimaced. It was a difficult and sad situation for everyone, including the patients' families.

His admiration for Macy stirred. In spite of the hell she'd gone through, she was a responsible woman and savvy federal agent.

The guard continued to run the footage, and Stone watched the sun rise outside, slanting across the gardens, then the grounds, until 9:10, when he saw someone inside Lynn's room at the window.

Slowly the camera caught the woman ripping the screen and cutting away enough of the mesh to crawl through.

A second later, she dropped to the ground outside. She lost her footing and hit the grass on her hands and knees, but quickly pushed up to stand. Still, she crouched low and inched away from the building.

"Zoom in on her face," Stone said.

The officer did as he said, and Stone's pulse jumped. He hadn't seen Macy's mother in years, and she'd definitely aged. Her dark hair was choppy as if she'd cut it herself, her eyes glassy-looking, her shirt inside out. She'd obviously dressed in a hurry. She kept glancing all around, scanning the gardens as she sneaked toward the woods bordering the property.

Time passed and a few patients and residents began to drift outside, gathering by the small pond and on the terrace where they enjoyed coffee, snacks, and board and card games. Each time one appeared, Mrs. Stark ducked behind a bush or tree.

Ten minutes later, she climbed the fence at the

edge of the woods, then she took off running and disappeared into the shadows.

No one had even noticed she was gone.

SADNESS NEARLY OVERPOWERED Macy as she studied the drawings of the monsters on her mother's wall. The disturbing sketches were obviously her mother's way of working out the demons in her mind.

The minimal furnishings in the room looked bleak as well. A single bed and wooden dresser. Plain white sheets and green comforter were tangled and twisted. Her pillow lay on the floor. She glanced inside the closet. A few pairs of sweatpants and jeans, T-shirts and long-sleeved shirts. Tennis shoes.

In the dresser drawer, she found plain underwear, socks and a couple of nightgowns. She rummaged through, searching for something to tell her more about her mother, but found nothing.

She returned to the wall of drawings, then sat down at the small desk. Charcoal and sketch paper had been placed on top, ready to use.

She opened the desk drawer and saw a journal inside. Pain squeezed her chest at her mother's random, disturbing drawings. One depicted a naked woman curled on the floor in the corner, her arms wrapped around her legs, her head bent into them as if she were crying.

She flipped to another page and saw a sketch of their house, night shadows casting an eerie feel over the trees and yard, with more monsters lurking in the woods.

Turning to the next page, she found a house again, this time with drawings of snakes climbing the walls and hanging from the roof. The next one depicted vultures attacking the windows. Then another one of bloody footprints on the floor of the wooden porch.

Were the bloody footprints delusions or pieces of memories?

Her phone buzzed. Stone.

"Macy," he said when she connected, "security footage shows your mother escaping through the window and running into the woods. There was no sign that anyone tried to break into her room or that someone assisted her in leaving."

"So she left on foot?"

"Yes. According to the time stamp, it was a little after nine. I got a copy if you want to look at it."

Did she? No, she trusted Stone. Macy glanced at her watch. It was noon now. Her mother had left three hours ago.

"I found a journal of her drawings," Macy said. "I think I may know where she's going."

"Where?" Stone asked.

Macy's stomach churned. "Home."

STONE ISSUED A BOLO for Macy's mother, then drove back to Briar Ridge. Macy sat silently beside him, staring out the window as if lost in another world. Armed with a new understanding of what she'd endured as a child and as an adult, it was no wonder she hadn't returned to Briar Ridge until the reunion. She had nothing good here to come back to.

He didn't blame her for wanting to leave again.

He had his own share of hurtful memories in Briar Ridge. That damn shooting. His brother's injury. His part in not seeing Ned Hodgkins's plans or the pain he was in from being bullied.

But he also had precious memories of fishing with his father and trailing after him when they went hiking. He'd known his father loved him.

That he loved the town. Hell, he'd lay down his life for his family and the residents of Briar Ridge.

Stone felt that responsibility now. He could never walk away from it. Never.

Still, he had a job to do, a case to solve. It would either bring closure for Macy or open up another can of worms that could destroy her life. "Did you learn anything from Dr. Garrett?"

Macy ran a hand over her ponytail. "Not much. It was early in my mom's therapy with her. I asked her to study the notes from their sessions for information about what might have happened at the house." Macy shrugged. "Who knows if it'll yield results? It's hard to know what's real and what's not in my mother's mind."

Stone didn't comment. That was more than she'd ever shared.

Macy turned to look out at the passing scenery, farmland, mountains, green grass and wildflowers dotting the mountain. All peaceful. Yet tension screamed off her, and there was nothing peaceful in her eyes.

He fought against the lump in his throat. "Did you find anything in the room?"

"Just sketches of monsters my mother drew," she said with a crack in her voice. "And the house. There were some of those."

Stone forced his hands to stay on the wheel when he wanted to take Macy's hand in his and comfort her. But that would be a mistake.

He had to keep his mind on the job.

"Let's drive by the house," Macy said. "My mother may have gone there."

"On foot that would take a while," Stone pointed out.

"But she could have stolen a car or hitched a ride."

"True."

He veered onto the turnoff for Main Street, and they fell silent as he drove to the Stark house. Macy's body was coiled with tension, dread in her eyes as he parked. The only car there was Macy's.

Still, they got out and approached the house slowly, then inched up the steps. Shadows cast dark spots about the house, the scent of death and mystery clinging to the dusty walls as they entered.

"I'll take the downstairs," Stone said.

Macy nodded, pausing to listen. The ticking of the clock and wind whistling through the eaves of the house echoed in the air.

He strode to the door to the basement while Macy combed the main floor and bedrooms.

Five minutes later, they met in the living room. "She's not here," he said.

"No, but she may be on her way," Macy said, her tone grim.

Stone's phone buzzed. His deputy, so he connected. "Yeah?"

"Sheriff, Gretta Wilson is here demanding to talk to you."

Dammit. Gretta had been a pain their backsides ever since high school. Stirring up gossip. Printing everyone's business no matter who she hurt.

If it was up to him, he'd lock her up.

But the first amendment and all the press hype prevented that.

When the blame went around for Ned Hodgkins's shooting tirade, he couldn't ignore the fact that she'd escalated the situation by exposing hurtful things the students had said about Ned.

Why was she at his office now? To make trouble? Get back at him and Macy for not giving her the scoop on Ned's son?

Or could she somehow have found out about the body?

TEN MINUTES LATER, Macy braced herself to remain unemotional as she and Stone climbed from his vehicle and walked toward the entrance to the sheriff's office. Gretta had gotten under her skin long ago, and she'd told her off in high school.

Needless to say they weren't friends and never would be.

Gretta's eyes lit up, and she made a beeline for them, blocking the doorway so they couldn't enter and shoving a microphone in their faces.

"Special Agent Macy Stark, is it true that a body was discovered at your family's home last night?"

Macy curled her hands into fists, wondering where Gretta had gotten her information. She swore the vile woman had cameras—or informants—everywhere.

But she couldn't avoid the inevitable or lie to the people in town, or that would make the situation worse. Taking a deep breath, she spoke calmly. "Yes, a body was discovered in the basement of the house where I grew up. At this time, we have not identified the remains, nor do we have any information to report about the cause of death or how long the body has been there."

Gretta narrowed her eyes. "But your mother lived in that house until recently, didn't she?"

"No comment."

Macy started to walk away, but Gretta stepped in her path. "Agent Stark, your mother suffers from mental illness, correct?"

Macy stiffened, but Stone cleared his throat. "This is Sheriff Stone Lawson. As Special Agent Stark stated, the police and FBI will be running a joint investigation into the situation. We have no further statement at the time."

Gretta opened her mouth to protest, but Stone gently brushed her aside, curved his arm around Macy's waist and hustled her toward the door.

Macy was trembling as they entered the sheriff's office. Mixed emotions pummeled her, and she spun toward Stone.

"I appreciate you trying to protect me, Stone, but

now Gretta will make something of you stepping in or hint that something is going on between us and make me look incompetent. I'm a professional. I can take care of myself."

STONE CROSSED HIS ARMS, his jaw tightening.

"Macy, your mother's medical history doesn't reflect on you. And no one is going to think you're unstable just because she was." And he had thought something was going on between them.

Or maybe that was his own wishful thinking.

Macy whirled around on him, hands on her hips. "Don't be naive, Stone. I heard the gossip growing up. Saw the way people looked at me in town when I was with her." Her voice cracked. "Even Brynn's mother didn't like that she and I were friends."

Anger shot through Stone at the unfairness of the situation. "Mrs. Gaines is a snob. Who cares what she thinks?"

But he saw it in her eyes. She cared. Because she'd been a little girl at the time. And in spite of the saying that words could never hurt you, they definitely could.

"I'm sorry," he said. "I don't mean to be insensitive." He heaved a breath. "I know people can be nasty. Judgmental even. But nothing your mother did or does can change who you are."

Macy squeezed her eyes closed for a moment and exhaled. When she opened them, she rubbed the back of her neck. "Sorry. I shouldn't let Gretta get to me."

"She's a troublemaker," Stone said wryly. He

reached for his phone. “I’m going to call the ME. See if she has any information.”

“Put her on Speaker,” Macy said.

He nodded, then rang the ME’s office. “Dr. Anderson, you’re on speaker with Agent Stark. Do you have anything on that body?”

“No ID yet. But the forensic anthropologist is using PMCT for identification and to determine cause of death.”

“Postmortem computed topography?” Macy asked.

“Exactly. It’s complicated, but in the case of skeletal remains, it analyzes toxicology, looks for traumatic fractures, surgical dissection of foreign bodies and state of carbonization to determine time, cause of death and previous injuries to the body.”

Stone pulled a hand down his chin. “And?”

“The body belongs to a male. Midthirties at time of death. Previous injuries include a broken nose, ribs and arm.”

“Someone beat him to death?” Stone asked.

“No, those were older injuries.”

“Then what was cause of death?” Macy asked.

“Puncture wounds and scoring on the bone indicate he was stabbed multiple times. Judging from the size and length of the scoring, it could have been done by a hunting knife or a common kitchen knife.”

Which her mother could have grabbed in the house. Macy remembered that one of the knives was missing when she was taking inventory of the kitchen. Remembered seeing an image of blood trickling down her arm…

"Ask the crime team if they found a kitchen knife that belongs to the set in the kitchen," she told Dr. Anderson.

His gaze met hers, then he nodded.

"Any guess as to how long he's been dead?" she asked the ME.

"Evidence suggests he was killed at least two decades ago, maybe twenty-five to twenty-seven years."

"So most likely he's been in that wall all that time?" Stone asked.

"Your forensics will have to determine that," Dr. Anderson said. "But there was no evidence that his body was frozen or kept somewhere else and moved there. We're running dental images and DNA results through the system to see if we can make an ID. Hopefully, we'll have more soon."

Stone thanked her, then ended the call. Macy rubbed her temple and sighed.

Stone gave her a sympathetic look. "You okay?"

She shook her head, her eyes pained. "If he's been dead that long and in that wall the whole time, my mother and I would have been living there."

Stone swallowed. He saw the wheels in her head spinning. If that was true, Macy's mother might know exactly what had happened.

Or...she might have murdered the man herself.

# *Chapter Seven*

Macy couldn't shake the conversation with Gretta. Stone had managed to hold her off, but that wouldn't last long. If Macy didn't find her mother soon, they'd need to run her picture on the news. Then everyone would know she'd escaped the Bear Mountain Gardens and that they considered her dangerous.

The hair on the back of her neck prickled as she and Stone found a booth at Daisy's Diner, a new place that had been built near the bookstore in town. The fifties decor boasted posters of old movies, red checkered tablecloths and a jukebox. With summer break for the schools and tourists returning to the area, it was packed with the lunch crowd today and teenagers chowing down on chili burgers and milkshakes.

Several locals turned to stare at them, whispering and talking in hushed tones. Obviously they'd seen the news and were wondering if a murderer was running loose in town.

The ME's estimated TOD for the man taunted her. It fit with the memory of the first time her mother had thrown her out in the rain.

The waitress, a perky brunette in her twenties with a nose ring, bobbed over to take their orders. Macy wasn't hungry but knew she needed fuel to do the job, so she ordered the special, a cup of Brunswick stew, and water while Stone ordered a loaded burger overflowing with mushrooms and a side of fries.

Mayor Gaines and his wife entered, the woman's cold stare a reminder of how she'd treated Macy as a child. The couple stopped at their table, the mayor's posture rigid.

"I saw your short briefing with that ghastly Gretta Wright," Mayor Gaines said. "Sheriff Lawson, when were you going to notify me that a murder had occurred in my town?"

A muscle ticked in Stone's jaw. "The skeletal remains were only discovered yesterday, Mayor. And I did plan to call you, but I wanted more information first."

"Yet you spoke with Ms. Wright?"

Stone took a long sip of his sweet iced tea. "I have no idea how or where Gretta got her information. And I certainly didn't intend to go public with this case until I clarified a few details."

The mayor buttoned his suit coat. "And have you?"

"As I said to the press, we've only begun the investigation. We don't have an ID on the body yet."

"And where did this murder occur?" the mayor asked.

"That's another question we're trying to answer."

"You're being evasive," the mayor said. "Tell me what you *do* know."

Stone glanced around, then lowered his voice.

"I'd rather not discuss this in a public place. There are eyes on us."

The mayor inhaled, then gave a clipped nod. But his wife shot daggers at Macy with her eyes. "Why am I not surprised that there was a dead man in your house?"

Macy's chest clenched. "Well, it came as a shock to me."

"Really? We all know your mother had problems. I heard you finally got her admitted to a hospital."

Macy tensed, but before she spoke, the mayor took his wife's arm. "Not here."

The waitress arrived with their food, and the mayor coaxed his wife to the back of the diner. Macy clutched her water, well aware everyone in the café was watching her and Stone.

Mrs. Gaines's rude comment was only the beginning. Once word spread about the body, she and her mother would be the center of a scandal that Macy wouldn't be able to escape.

STONE WANTED TO throttle the mayor's wife. If he hadn't thought it would embarrass Macy, he would have told the woman off.

Anxious to leave, he and Macy finished their meal in silence. He grabbed the bill and paid it before Macy could, then stood and followed her to the door. But as they stepped outside, Kate McKendrick and Brynn Gaines appeared.

Macy halted, her eyes widening as Kate enveloped her in a hug. "We were going to stop by the house and see if you needed help later," Kate said.

Brynn rolled her wheelchair closer and took Macy's hand. "You okay, Macy? We saw the news."

Emotions flickered in Macy's eyes, and she took a breath. "Yes, but it's a mess. I'll be staying in town until we solve this case."

"Who was the man?" Kate asked.

Macy and Stone exchanged a look. "I can't talk about it here. I'll explain everything later."

Kate and Brynn murmured their understanding, although Stone saw the worry in their eyes. The three had been like sisters growing up. Different personalities but inseparable. Brynn's mother pushed her into beauty pageants and focused on appearances while Kate had been shy and bookish.

When her mother died in the shooting, Kate understandably had a difficult time. But she'd become a teacher and now was the high school principal.

Brynn had suffered as well. Surgery and physical therapy weren't able to repair the damage from the bullet she'd taken and she was partially paralyzed. Mrs. Gaines had smothered her, but after the reunion, he'd heard Brynn moved into her own place.

He was glad the reunion had brought the three women back together. Macy was going to need her friends now.

Rain clouds rolled across the sky, obliterating the midday sun and hinting at a summer storm as they got in his car. Macy remained silent as he started the engine.

"Take me back to the house so I can get my car," Macy said.

"Listen, Macy, I'll go with you to your house."

She shook her head. “I need some time alone, Stone. Or don’t you trust me? Do you think I’m going to try to hide something from you?”

The edge to her voice made his jaw tighten. “That’s not what I meant. But I understand you’re close to this case.”

Macy gritted her teeth. “I am, but I also know my mother can be dangerous. If she shows up, I’ll keep her there until you arrive.” She gave a look of gratitude. “I need you working every clue.”

He reluctantly agreed, then his phone buzzed, and he saw it was his deputy so he answered. “Sheriff, I got a call about a stolen car. Thought you might want to check it out in case the Stark woman was involved.”

“I’ll be right there.”

“What was that about?” Macy asked as he headed toward the inn.

Stone decided not to share unless he knew something, so he shrugged it off. “Just routine stuff.”

If Mrs. Stark had stolen the car and he had to chase her down, he didn’t want Macy to have to be part of it.

When he parked, he caught her arm before she got out. “Even though the crime team is finished, Macy, you know what all was there. Be alert for something they might have missed.”

Her eyes darkened, then she got out without responding.

YELLOW CRIME SCENE tape flapped in the wind, the dark rain clouds hovering above the house a grim reminder that Macy’s home was now the scene of a homicide investigation. She parked in front of the dilapidated structure, wondering if she should just have it demolished once she solved the mystery of what happened in that basement. The property had some value but not the house, especially with its sordid history now.

Senses alert in case her mother had found her way back, she scanned the front and side yard, then climbed from her car and walked up to the porch. The front door was unlocked, the screen door banging back and forth.

The rickety stairs creaked as she walked up them, and a screeching sound echoed from somewhere inside. Pulling her gun at the ready, she inched into the house. Fingerprint dust covered everything in sight, including the doorways and knob and what little was left of the furnishings.

It looked as if the place had been tossed. But that was partly her doing, partly the forensic team. She'd been rushing like a madwoman to clean out the house so she could hightail it out of town. No telling how long she'd have to stay in Briar Ridge and endure the gossip and stares now. More painful memories would pile up on top of the ones she'd tried to forget since she'd left Briar Ridge. And if her mother was guilty of murder…

The screeching sound jarred her gaze toward the kitchen and back door. Slowly she crept through the living room and looked inside the kitchen. The stench of cat pee hit her, and she spotted the source of the screeching. A stray cat was clawing at the back screen door to get out.

Breathing out in relief, she hurried to open the

door. The feral cat hissed at her, then darted outside the minute she opened it. She watched it race into the woods to escape and wished she could do the same.

She reached for the door to close it but caught sight of a shadowy figure moving through the rows of thick pines. Thunder suddenly crackled, and a streak of lightning lit the sky.

Macy hated storms, but she stepped outside, desperate to see who the person was. Dark clothing, hunched over, hugging the trees like an animal. She rushed down the steps, but the figure turned and darted through the woods, disappearing into the shadows of the weeds and brush.

Her heart hammered. Was that her mother?

STONE FLIPPED OFF the siren on his police car as he came to a stop in the RV park.

This place was a popular spot for tourists on a budget who wanted the benefits of the creek and proximity to the hiking trails and canoeing. Except for the rumble of thunder and a dog barking, the wooded area was quiet.

A big guy who looked like a lumberjack stood from where he and a boy about ten were playing horseshoes beside the RV. They both halted when they saw his police car, and the man walked toward him.

"Sheriff Lawson," he said.

"Abel and Matt Young," the lumberjack guy said.

"My deputy said you reported a car missing."

The man nodded and gestured to his son to gather the horseshoes. "Yeah, last night we went camping over on the mountain. When we got back this morning, my Jeep was gone."

He scratched his beard. "First I thought the wife took it into town with my little girl for supplies. But she said she went for a hike to the falls with Jordie, and when she got back, the Jeep was gone."

"What time was that?"

The man glanced at his watch. "Sometime around noon." He pulled a face of disgust. "We picked this place because we thought it was safe to raise a family. Now…not so sure."

Stone hated the distrust crime caused. The shooting years ago had completely divided the town and made everyone suspicious and wary of their neighbors.

"I'm sorry this happened to you," Stone said sincerely. "I will do everything possible to recover your vehicle and get to the bottom of it."

"I appreciate that," the man said. "My wife is a nervous wreck. She wants to pack up and go back to Durham where her mama lives." He gestured toward his son. "But Matt loves it out here."

Stone remembered hiking, fishing and canoeing with Mickey and his own father and nodded. "For what it's worth, I do think you're safe. And if you want, I can help you arrange for a rental car." He glanced around the RV park searching for security cameras. But there were none out here in the wilderness.

"I appreciate it. But we've already contacted our insurance company and they're sending over a rental."

"You gave my deputy the make, model and license of the Jeep?"

"We did," he said.

"We'll get an APB issued for it. I'll let you know if or when it turns up."

The man thanked him, and they shook hands, then Stone headed back to his squad car, considering the possibilities. Some kids could have stolen the vehicle, looking for a joyride.

But considering the proximity to Bear Mountain Gardens, it was possible Macy's mother had made it on foot here and stolen the Jeep. If so and she was headed home, she might already be there.

He pulled his phone to call Macy and warn her.

MACY'S PULSE HAMMERED as she jogged toward the woods to give chase. The clouds opened up, dumping rain, and lightning flashed, striking a tree in the distance. Her phone was ringing on her belt, but she ignored it and fought through the rain to reach the edge of the woods.

Rain pummeled her, the thick downpour clogging her vision and slowing her as the wind picked up and blew leaves and debris around her. She zigzagged through the massive line of trees, weaving back and forth in search of the shadowy figure. But it had disappeared.

Heaving a breath, she wiped rain from her face and trudged on. Her shoes sank into the muddy ground as she dodged a falling limb and jumped over twigs that snapped off from the force of the wind.

She ran half a mile, searching, looking, stopping to examine the brush, but the heavy downpour made it impossible to track. Frustrated, she halted and turned, scanning all directions, but everything was a foggy blur.

Another crack of lightning and a tree falling in the woods made her turn and jog back to the house.

Battling the storm took all her energy and by the time she arrived at the house, rain drenched her clothing and hair, and she felt chilled to the bone. She rushed up the back steps and into the house to escape the weather, then checked her phone. A voice mail from Stone.

"Car stolen within five miles of Bear Mountain Gardens. Issued an APB. Be on the lookout for a 2020 Jeep Cherokee. Navy blue."

Her mother could have escaped and stolen the car and be here now.

She hurried to the front door. The headlights of a dark sedan nearly blinded her, and she froze, a hand on her gun as she waited to see who was behind the wheel.

SHE WATCHED THE HOUSE, a fine sheen of sweat coating her skin. Macy was back in town. And she'd found a body in the damn house.

She'd heard the news in the car on the way out here. At this point, the police knew nothing. It had to stay that way.

But Macy was FBI now. What if she figured out what happened?

What if she remembered?

Fighting panic, she opened her pill bottle, popped a Xanax into her mouth and swallowed it down.

She couldn't take that chance.

# *Chapter Eight*

Macy clenched her weapon and started outside to confront whoever was in that car, but as soon as she stepped onto the porch the vehicle moved on.

Probably just some rubbernecker wanting to see the house where a dead body was just discovered.

Breathing out in relief, she went back inside and closed the door. Dammit, this place was spooking her.

She wanted to be done with it. But that couldn't happen until she learned the truth. Deciding to take another look around in case she'd missed something, she hurried to her mother's room and searched beneath the bed, then the closet again. She stood on tiptoe and raked her hand along the top shelf and her finger brushed something. She strained to reach it but couldn't so she dragged the desk chair in the corner to the closet and climbed up on it. Shining her flashlight across the shelf, she saw a photo album and a box.

She pulled them both down, set the box on the floor, then sank into the chair to look through them. First the photo album. Macy had never seen the album before. She had no idea her mother had even kept one. Lynn Stark hadn't exactly been the sentimental, doting mother.

Her mother had refused to tell her anything about her father. Macy had long ago decided it didn't matter. If he'd wanted to be part of her life, he would have.

But if he'd stayed in touch, he might know what happened here. Maybe she'd find a clue in here, a picture or a love letter.

She opened the book and found dozens of pictures of her when she was an infant. She was swaddled in a pink blanket and wore a big pink bow. In other pictures, she was in a crib with purple polka-dot sheets and a stuffed bear propped in the corner. She flipped the pages, surprised that her mother had chronicled her development.

There was her first Christmas where she was sitting on Santa's lap, then Easter in a pretty yellow dress and bonnet. Her first birthday where she'd dug her whole pudgy little hand into the cake. And Halloween when she dressed up like a unicorn.

The pictures continued, marking her first year, then second, third and fourth. The day she'd gotten her first soccer ball, her jump rope, swinging at the park, her first missing tooth.

Her heart stuttered at the sight of a picture of her mother cradling her and rocking her. The tender look on her mother's face was not one Macy remembered.

But her eyes glowed with love and affection.

A well of sadness opened up inside Macy, and

tears blurred her eyes. Macy struggled to recall those moments when she looked happy and loved. But the pictures stopped abruptly at age five, and so had any pleasant memories.

Had her mother loved her at one time?

If so, what had happened to make her stop?

STONE CLENCHED HIS jaw as the interview with him and Macy replayed on the news. That damn Gretta Wright was such a pain in the butt. He hoped she didn't destroy Macy.

"Police are now looking for a 2020 navy blue Jeep Cherokee which was stolen this afternoon from an RV park. They suspect that a woman named Lynn Stark took the vehicle after escaping the psychiatric facility where she is undergoing treatment. Ms. Stark owns the house where the body was found in the wall by her daughter, Special Agent Macy Stark, and is wanted for questioning in what they believe was a homicide."

He glanced at his deputy. "Where the hell does she get her information?"

Murphy shrugged, then looked back at his computer. "People talk. Can't hide the truth from the public."

Stone narrowed his eyes. "Did you tell her?"

His deputy shook his head. "It's a small town, Sheriff. The residents have a right to know if a criminal is on the streets."

Stone stiffened. "First of all, we don't know that Lynn Stark had anything to do with the corpse or even with the murder itself. And we are not going to accuse someone publicly without evidence."

Murphy made a clicking sound with his teeth. "All the more reason to use every resource to get the word out so we can find her."

His lungs squeezed for air. Murphy was right, although sympathy for Macy welled inside him.

*You can't let that stop you from doing your job.*

"You think Macy knows what happened and just isn't talking?" Murphy asked.

Stone swallowed hard. "The man has been dead over twenty-five years," he said. "Macy would have been a little girl then. So no, I don't think she knows. She was in shock when she called me and I got to the house."

The chair creaked as Murphy leaned back in it. "Maybe so. But the real question is would she cover for her now? For all we know, she could help her mother hide out. With her experience as an agent, she'd know how to do it."

Stone didn't like the direction of the conversation. "Do not go around stirring up those kinds of questions," he snapped. "Macy has enough on her shoulders without gossip."

"I'm not," Murphy said. "But people are going to wonder."

Stone's temper flared. His deputy was right. But he didn't like it. "Because she's had psychological issues, she also would be a good scapegoat."

"True," Murphy said. "But hard to believe she was living in that house and didn't know a dead man was in the wall."

"Let's just concentrate on doing the job and finding her," Stone said.

Hopefully Forensics would have something useful to add, too. Concrete evidence, not just speculation.

His gut churned as he stood. He didn't like the doubts creeping through his mind. Macy did have secrets. And a troubled past with her mother.

She'd gone to the house, and he hadn't heard back from her. What if her mother had shown up?

He had no idea if she'd hurt Macy or not.

He pulled his keys from his pocket. He'd take a ride out there and see what was happening.

EMOTIONS CLOGGED HER throat as Macy closed the photo album. There was nothing of her father inside, although now she knew that at one time her mother had a tender side for her.

Next she opened the box and realized it held items from her childhood. The pink baby blanket. The little white teddy bear. Several hair bows, frilly socks and a pair of black patent leather toddler shoes.

Faded tissue paper had been wrapped around other items. She pulled it away and found two dresses that looked as if they'd been hand smocked.

A memory tickled her conscience—her mother humming along with the buzz of a sewing machine. Fabric swatches littering a table. Her standing on the table while her mother pinned the hem of the Easter dress she was making.

The memory disappeared as quickly as it had

come, and an image of her mother screaming at her because she spilled milk on the floor took shape. Then her mother threatening to spank her with a switch she cut from the cherry tree out back. She was six at the time, and she'd run and hidden in the closet, terrified of a beating.

A knock on the front door startled her, and she set the dresses back inside the box and hurried to the living room. She half hoped it was her mother so they could talk, but her mother wouldn't knock. And if she was on the run and off her meds, she might be incoherent.

Bracing herself in case it was her and she was in one of her irrational states, she checked through the window.

Stone stood on the other side. "Macy?"

Relieved, she exhaled and opened the door. The rain had stopped, but the sky was still dark, the clouds ominous, and the wind shook raindrops from the trees.

"Did you find that Jeep?" Macy asked.

"Not yet. Gretta is running it on the news."

Her mouth tightened at the mention of the reporter's name. "I thought I saw someone in the woods earlier and gave chase but didn't catch up. If it was my mother, she could have parked the Jeep somewhere and then sneaked up through the back."

"We'll find it and her," Stone assured her as he stepped inside.

"There was also a sedan that slowed in front of the drive. I didn't see the driver, so it may have been nothing. But she could have ditched the Jeep and changed vehicles."

Stone shifted. "Did you get the license plate of the sedan?"

"It was too dark, and the lights were blinding." She shrugged. "Of course since the news ran, there's bound to be curiosity seekers driving by. And with school on summer break, I half expect teenagers to try to come in and get a peek. Just the kind of dare they might pull."

"True. I can post a guard here if you want to protect the property."

Macy scrunched her nose, considering it. "I don't think that's necessary. There's nothing valuable here. But maybe the night deputy should do routine drive-bys to prevent vandalism or in case my mother shows up."

"I'll put him on it," Stone agreed. "You know you can't stay here. Now the news aired, if your mother didn't kill the man, whoever did could come back."

"I know. I'm going to take another look downstairs and then head to the inn for the night."

Stone's eyes darkened. "You sure you want to do that?"

"I have to make sure we didn't miss anything."

He studied her for a long minute. "I'll go downstairs with you."

Reluctantly she agreed. Clenching her flashlight with a clammy hand, she inhaled a deep breath and made her way to the basement door. The wood floor creaked as Stone followed her down the rickety stairs. The stench of death blended with the moldy smell, and she had to drag in a breath to stem the nausea.

"If this man has been here over twenty-five years, you would have been about five to eight years old at the time," Stone said out loud.

Macy nodded, but his voice faded as the sudden sound of pouring rain beat down and she was launched back in time.

"MACY?" STONE STUDIED HER pale face, then quickly realized her mind was somewhere else.

"My mother never let me come down here," she said in a distant voice. "She kept it locked and said it was off-limits."

"Did she explain why?" Stone asked.

She shook her head, reached the bottom of the staircase, then paused and stared at the hole in the wall.

The plaster had been rotting when she'd found the body, but after dusting it for prints and taking trace samples, it had been ripped apart in sections for the recovery team to remove the skeleton.

"Just that there were rats down here," Macy murmured.

Maybe she had meant human ones.

"I used to have nightmares about them crawling through the eaves of the house and vents and dropping from the ceiling."

Stone held his tongue. While Macy had been having nightmares, he'd been camping and fishing with his father and Mickey. They'd had a good childhood with loving parents until the high school shooting blew up their lives.

The urge to comfort Macy tugged at him. "Maybe she was protecting you by warning you away from down here."

"Maybe," Macy said, although she didn't sound convinced, making him wonder what secrets she'd kept.

The ties between parent and child ran strong. Kids craved love and would forgive and forget in order to get it. Some children of abusive parents or ones with addictions and mental diseases often lied to cover for their folks. He'd seen it on the job a couple of times on domestic calls when he'd had to call social services, and he felt for those kids.

Had Macy lied and covered for hers? Would she do so again now if she thought her mother was guilty of murder?

"You said you didn't know your father, didn't you?" he asked quietly.

"I didn't," Macy said. "She never told me his name. I assumed if he didn't want me, why should I care?"

As much as she presented a tough front, he heard the hurt in her voice. Not knowing had to have eaten at her.

"Have you seen your birth certificate?"

"Yeah, I found it in the desk. But my father's name is not listed on it."

"Was your mother always ill?"

Macy looked at him, confusion in her eyes. "I

thought so, at least as far back as I can remember. But…now I don't know."

"Why do you say that?"

Macy heaved a breath. "Because I found a photo album filled with pictures of me when I was little. Shots of me on holidays and birthdays and one of her holding me with love in her eyes."

Dammit. Not only had her father been absent and she'd thought he didn't want her, but she'd thought her mother didn't love her.

"I'm sorry, Macy. It sounds like you had it really hard…"

She lifted her chin. "I don't want your sympathy, Stone. I want to know what the hell happened. I can't leave here until I do."

## *Chapter Nine*

Macy battled her emotions. Kate was the only one who'd ever witnessed her mother's erratic behavior and how terrified she'd been as a child.

Exposing her painful secrets to Stone made her feel more vulnerable than she'd ever felt in her life.

But she had to face the truth, no matter what it was.

If her mother was guilty of homicide, she'd deal with it. If she was innocent, she needed Macy's help.

"Your mother was young back then. Did she have a boyfriend or date anyone?"

"You heard the rumors," Macy said. "My mother was crazy. What man would want to deal with that?"

Stone walked over and rubbed her arm, forcing her to look at him. "I know she was troubled, Macy. But that doesn't mean she didn't have male friends. Even if it was no one serious, do you remember a man coming around here? Someone she may have been involved with, even if it was just for a night or two here and there?"

Macy rubbed her temple. "She did bring a couple of men home, but I never met them." Because her mother had either locked her in the closet or thrown her outside while she entertained.

"Did she leave you with a sitter or go out when you were playing at a friend's?"

Macy's throat closed. "I didn't have playdates, Stone. At five, my mother was a mess. When she was home, she didn't spend time with me or drive me to see a friend. And I never wanted anyone to come over."

A muscle ticked in his jaw. "Because you didn't want them to see what was going on?"

"Exactly." Refusing to keep diving into her humiliating past, she turned and ran up the stairs. The only one who knew and had seen the truth was Kate.

But soon everyone was going to know.

STONE FOLLOWED MACY back up the stairs to the kitchen and found her leaning her hands on the counter and drawing in a deep breath.

"I know this is difficult," he said. "We should call it a night and start fresh tomorrow."

She nodded. "Maybe the ME will have an ID on the body then."

"Hopefully so." Then he could get to the bottom of this case and give Macy some peace. Only finding the truth might do the opposite.

"Did your mom have any close friends she might have confided in?"

Macy made a wry sound. "I don't remember her having any friends. Ever."

"How about her folks?"

"My grandparents died before I was born."

So Macy had had no one except an unstable mother.

"What about a job?"

"She managed to put food on the table by cleaning houses for folks around town."

"Do you know who she worked for?"

Macy shook her head. "I heard her mention a couple of names. But she kept a calendar somewhere to keep up with her jobs. I think I saw it when I was cleaning out her things."

"Did you throw it away?"

"No. There were other papers in there and I decided I'd tackle it later in case there was something important in the paperwork." She went to the desk in the corner, opened the top drawer and removed a folder and then several day planners. They dated back fifteen years but stopped about five years ago.

"Let me take these and I'll make a list of names of people we can talk to," Macy said.

"Let's divide them," Stone suggested. "We can meet tomorrow and start following up."

Macy hesitated. "If you don't mind, I'd like to look through them myself first. There might be something in there that will jog my memories."

Stone shifted onto the balls of his feet. "As long as you share what you find, Macy."

Anger flared in her eyes. "Don't worry. I intend to face whatever happens."

Stone wanted to reach out and comfort her. But held his hand back. "It's natural to have allegiance to your mother," he said softly.

Pain streaked Macy's face. "It's complicated," Macy said. "But I'll do whatever needs to be done."

He gave a nod. He just hoped the truth didn't destroy her.

THE NEXT MORNING Macy got up early and skimmed through the calendars her mother had kept, jotting down the names of the people her mother had cleaned for. She had no idea how many of them still lived in Briar Ridge, but there were seven names within a five-year time span of when the man in the wall would have been murdered, so she focused on those first.

She needed to discuss the list with Stone, but first she met Kate and Brynn for breakfast at Daisy's Diner. Whispers and stares told her that the rumor mill hadn't missed a beat. And now she and her mysterious mother and their connection to a murder were at the heart of it.

Her friends had already ordered a pot of coffee and platter of assorted pastries for the table. They both gave her tentative smiles when she slid into the booth to join them.

"How are you doing?" Kate asked as Macy poured herself a cup of coffee from the pot.

"As well as I can," Macy said honestly.

Brynn stirred sweetener into her tea. "Did you get any sleep?"

Macy shrugged. "Not much." And when she'd finally drifted off, she'd had fitful nightmares of the bones and the man's deep, hollow eye sockets.

"Why don't you come and stay with me while you're here?" Kate offered.

Macy shook her head. "I'm not going to impose on either of you," Macy said. "Besides, aren't you and Riggs planning your wedding?"

A sheepish grin tugged at Kate's mouth. "We're starting to," Kate admitted. "We've set a date for end of summer and decided to have it outdoors at the Bear Mountain Resort."

"That's so exciting," Macy said. "I'm really happy for you."

Brynn squeezed Kate's shoulder. "You deserve it, Kate."

Kate pulled both their hands into hers. "We all deserve to be happy. And Macy, you could never impose. We're spit sisters, remember?"

A blush climbed Macy's neck as she recalled the three of them spitting into their hands and rubbing them together. "Thanks, both of you. But I'm okay, really. I'm staying at the inn, which is lovely now it's been redone. And part of that is due to you, Kate, and the rebuilding of the high school."

Kate looked sheepish. "I'm just glad folks in town are renovating and sprucing up their businesses. The town has been depressed for too long."

"I hope finding this body doesn't send everyone back into a spin," Macy said.

"Don't worry about that," Brynn said. "Just tell us how we can help."

Macy squeezed their hands, then thanked them and reached for her coffee, inhaling the rich pecan scent. They all dived into the pastries then as more customers slipped into the diner. Two older women stared at her while a couple of her former classmates she'd seen at the recent reunion gave her sympathetic looks.

She ignored them and finished her coffee, anxious to leave. "I'm meeting Stone at his office in a few minutes," she said as she waved the waitress over for the check. "Last night I found my mother's cleaning calendar. We're going to talk to her employers and see if she shared personal information with them."

Kate grabbed the check and wagged her finger at Macy, indicating she was covering the bill. "Do you have any idea who the dead man is?"

"Not yet," Macy said. "You know my mother never had a serious boyfriend."

"But she brought men home sometimes, didn't she?" Kate asked.

Macy shuddered. "A few times, but I stayed away from them."

Brynn bit down on her bottom lip. "Macy, I hate to suggest this, but…do you think it could be your father? That maybe he came by one night and he and your mother argued, and something happened between them?"

STONE DROPPED BY to check on his brother on the way to his office. But Mickey slammed the door in his face and told him to butt out of his business. He also smelled like booze again.

A sense of foreboding overcame him. He was losing his little brother. Hell, he'd been losing him for years.

And he had no idea what to do about it.

Gray rain clouds drifted across the sky as he parked at the sheriff's office. The moment he stepped inside, his deputy looked up at him. "Tip came in. That stolen Jeep was spotted at a gas station near the motel off the main highway. I was going to check it out."

"Go home and get some rest. I know you did drive-bys last night at the Stark house. See anything?"

Murphy shook his head. "Just a couple of teenage boys looking through the windows. I warned 'em that place is a crime scene and if they or any of their friends went inside, I'd lock 'em up."

Murphy was a big guy with a deep baritone voice. Couple that with his badge and gruff exterior, he could put the fear of God in someone with just one look.

Stone thanked him, then texted Macy about the Jeep. She responded saying she'd be there in five minutes, so he went to his office and phoned the ME. "Dr. Anderson, do you have an ID for me?"

"Not yet," she said. "I sent DNA to the lab and am waiting on results. I'll let you know as soon as I do."

He pulled up the CSI team's report and skimmed their notes. Several pairs of fingerprints upstairs, only two downstairs. Hair and fibers of various sorts, which were being analyzed. No guns in the house. They had found the knife set on the kitchen counter and were analyzing those for blood, but they had not found the missing knife.

Was that the murder weapon?

A knock sounded, then Macy poked her head in the doorway. "Stone?"

"Yeah, let's go." He stood, grabbed his keys and they rushed outside to his squad car.

"Where is the Jeep?" Macy asked.

"It was spotted at a gas station near a motel on

the highway heading toward Bear Mountain Resort." The morning sun splintered through the storm clouds, beating down on the pavement.

Families were already gathering at the park, kids playing chase on the playground, walkers and joggers taking advantage of the temperature before the heat rose today. Already signs had been posted advertising the Fourth of July parade and festival planned for the holiday celebration. Arts-and-crafts booths, face painting for the children, a bicycle parade for kids who decorated their bikes, floats, and food trucks would provide entertainment for the day, and a stage had been set up for music guests. Come dark, they would have a fireworks show.

He flipped on his siren to maneuver past the slower traffic. If Macy's mother was in that Jeep, and if she'd seen the news, she might be on her way out of town. They passed farmland as he exited the city limits and he wound around the mountain road for three miles, then turned right at the fork onto the highway leading toward the resort.

Another mile down the road, and he reached the gas station. It was connected to a convenience store, but the Jeep was not in the parking lot.

"She could be miles and miles from here by now," Macy said.

Stone parked and opened his car door. "Let's go see what the store clerk has to say."

Macy got out and they walked up to the door together, then went inside. A family with toddler twins was checking out at the register, armed with fruit drinks and snacks. Stone waited until they finished paying, then stepped up to the register. A kid in his twenties with a tattoo of a tiger on his forearm looked up at them.

Stone identified himself. "I got a call that someone spotted at 2020 navy blue Jeep here."

"Yeah, that was me," the kid said. "Saw on the news you were looking for it."

"When was it you saw the Jeep?"

"Last night about six. But I didn't see the news till this morning. Soon as I did, I called."

"Did you see who was driving it?" Macy asked.

The young man tugged at his earring. "Looked like a woman, but I didn't see her face. Gassed up, used the john and sped away."

The bell on the door tinkled and another family entered, fanning out to comb the aisles for their beverage and snack choices. A guy in his forties followed them in, walked straight to the refrigerated section and grabbed a twelve-pack of beer.

"Do you have security cameras?" Stone asked.

The boy coughed into his hands. "No, manager said we don't need 'em."

You never needed them until there was a crime, Stone thought wryly.

"Which direction did the driver go when she left?" Macy said.

The kid pointed north toward the resort and the stretch where he knew there was a motel, and Stone and Macy hurried to his car. Stone peeled from the parking lot knowing every minute counted.

If Macy's mother had stayed at the motel, maybe she was still there.

# *Chapter Ten*

Macy's nerves teetered on the edge as Stone sped north. The mountains rose with stiff peaks and ridges; rustic cabins and houses perched on hills that overlooked the creek and river.

The motel looked outdated and sat off the road near a truck stop. Mud splattered the concrete structure, and the low windows were coated with grime.

She cringed at the idea of her mother staying here, hiding out like a common criminal.

Stone parked in front of the motel entrance, and she scanned the parking lot. Two pickup trucks, a Range Rover, another truck with a pop-up camper and a mini-van. The navy blue Jeep was parked at the end of the row of motel rooms in plain sight.

"Stay in the car," Stone said softly. "Let me handle this."

She shook her head and reached for the door handle. "If my mother is here, she might respond better to me than you."

His brows arched as if he wondered if she was playing him, but he refrained from expressing his doubts out loud.

"Let's split up," she said. "Go talk to the desk clerk, see what you can find out and get a key. I'll stake out the room in case she's holed up in there and spots us and tries to run."

"Are you sure about this, Macy?" Stone asked.

Her gaze met his, the questions in his eyes haunting her. She thought she'd earned his trust and respect when they'd worked together recently, but if she were in his shoes, she might ask the same questions.

"I'm not going to let her get away or help her escape," she said. "I told you. I want to know what happened in that house." And if her mother was a murderer.

He exhaled, then headed for the entrance. Macy shut the car door as quietly as possible, then eased toward the front side of the building and crept along the wall of rooms. Two families exited their rooms, children chatting excitedly about their plans to go swimming for the day.

Senses honed, she glanced all around her and inside the rooms with open curtains and saw two rooms were empty. In the other one, a couple was watching TV. She crept toward the Jeep and peeked inside, but there was no one in the vehicle. The Jeep belonged to a family who'd been camping, and hiking gear had been stowed in the back.

Nothing to indicate her mother had been in there. Although her mother had run from her room to escape, and they had no indication that she'd taken anything with her.

She moved to the next room and noted the curtains were closed so she couldn't see inside. Knowing there were no back door exits, she raised her fist and knocked on the door. "Housekeeping."

She stepped to the side of the door, tapping her foot as she waited and listening for sounds of someone inside. The cheap rooms had window air conditioners, and the hum of it was so loud that if anyone were inside, the machine might drown out the sound.

"Housekeeping, I have clean towels," she said as she knocked again.

Again no one answered, so she jiggled the door, but it was locked.

She decided to try a different tactic and knocked once more. "Mom, it's me, Macy. If you're in there, please open up."

STONE IDENTIFIED HIMSELF to the desk clerk, a sixty-something man named Everett. His gray hair was thinning; his teeth were stained yellow from years of smoking, his hands pocked with age spots.

"We had a call about that navy Jeep out there," Stone said. "It was stolen yesterday. Did you see who was driving it?"

The man adjusted his thick Coke-bottle glasses. "Some lady, I think."

Stone showed him a picture of Macy's mother, although it was an older photo Macy had given him when the woman was ten years younger. "Was this the woman?"

Everett squinted as he studied it. "I can't say for sure. Eyes ain't what they used to be."

Judging from the man's thick glasses, Stone had expected as much. "How about checking the registry? The woman we're looking for is Lynn Stark."

He ran a hand over his bald spot, then glanced at the registry. "Don't see that name here."

"She could have checked in under a different name. Look for a woman traveling alone."

He checked again, then shook his head. "Got a couple of families and group of hikers. Four empty rooms." He tapped the desk with his finger. "Oh, someone did report a noise in room eight on the end, but nobody was in that room."

Ms. Stark could have broken in and spent the night there.

"Can I take a look at that room?"

"I reckon so." He hobbled around the desk with a metal key ring. He handed Stone the keys. "I'd show you, but my arthritis is acting up this morning. Knees hurting. Just bring the keys back when you're finished."

Stone nodded, then took the ring of keys and strode back outside. He glanced at each room as he passed but saw nothing suspicious although decided to check the empty ones after he looked in room eight.

He found Macy outside the room. "No single female registered. Desk clerk said there was a noise in this room last night but no one registered."

"I knocked but no one answered," Macy said.

Stone inserted the key and turned the lock. The door squeaked as he opened it and looked inside. At first glance, no one was inside.

Macy crept into the doorway and flipped on a light. The room was early eighties decor with a queen bed draped in an orange floral bedspread that was tangled from where someone had slept in it.

"Someone was here," Macy said.

"Looks that way." Stone strode to the bathroom and glanced inside. "Whoever was here took a shower. Towel is wet, and shampoo and soap have been used."

Macy heaved a breath. "If it was my mom, she broke in and slept here last night. Then she ditched the Jeep."

"There's one way to find out," Stone said. "I'll call a forensic team to dust for prints."

Macy rubbed her temple. "The question is—where is she now?"

WHILE THE CSI team processed room eight, Macy and Stone checked the other rooms but found nothing suspicious. She told the investigator to compare DNA and prints from the room to the ones at her mother's house.

On the way back to town, Macy and Stone stopped at Pearl's Pie & Dine for lunch and to plan their next move. Macy ordered the special, chicken and dumplings, while Stone ordered meat loaf, then they finished off the meal with fresh peach cobbler and vanilla ice cream.

"Did you look through your mother's calendars?" Stone asked.

Macy washed the delicious, sweet fruity dessert down with coffee, then pulled the list of names from her phone.

"Yes. I made a list of people she was working for around the time of the man's death," she said. "There are eight names, but I don't know how many of these folks still live around Briar Ridge."

"Let's go through them, and I'll see if I can help."

Macy took another sip of coffee before she began. "First there's a woman named Beverly Jones."

"Miss Beverly still lives on Main Street," Stone said. "She's in her seventies now, sings in the church choir, makes blankets for the children's hospital."

"She sounds special," Macy said.

"Yeah, everyone in town loves her." Stone pushed his empty plate away and wiped his mouth. "Who else?"

"Pat and Ken Dansing."

"They moved away years ago to Charleston, South Carolina, to be closer to their daughter and her family. If we need to, I can find a way to get in touch with them."

Macy shrugged. "May be worth a phone call. Next is Troy and Shirley Cregan."

"Troy and Shirley run the local butcher shop."

Macy nodded. "Dodie Lewis?"

"Sorry to say Dodie passed away a while back. Cancer."

Macy deleted her name. "What about Loretta Pruitt?"

Stone whistled. "Loretta's still around. She used to run the day care in town, but she's retired now."

"Vicki Germaine?"

"Property manager for those cabins on the creek."

Macy drummed her fingers on the table. "Last one is Adeline and Prentice Walkman." Macy hesitated. "Prentice Walkman—he's running for senate, isn't he?"

Stone pulled a hand down his chin. "Yes. They haven't lived here in ages. Sad story there. They had a son, but he got hit by a car when he was seven. They moved after that. I guess it was just too painful for them to stay."

"I can understand that," Macy said. After all, she'd run from Briar Ridge to escape her own painful memories.

STONE PAID THE bill and drove Macy to Beverly Jones's house, a small craftsman bungalow that looked as inviting as the sweet lady who lived there.

She leaned on her cane as she opened the door and invited them in, then offered them iced tea, but he was still full from lunch and Macy politely declined.

She led them through the entryway past a craft room to the right where shelves held baskets of colorful yarn and a table was laden with blankets she'd already knitted for the hospital. The living room was cozy with a couch and a rocking chair, which was where Ms. Beverly sat, her knitting needles and a work in progress in the basket beside the chair.

Her wavy hair was white, her body trim, her smile tentative as if she knew the reason for their visit.

"I saw the news." Beverly's eyes glimmered with compassion when she looked at Macy. "I know you've been through a lot, dear. That must have been some shock."

"It was," Macy said softly. "We're trying to figure out what happened. I found a list of people my mother used to clean for and your name was on it. I was hoping you could tell me more about her."

Beverly picked up the blanket and began working the knitting needles as if she needed to do something with her hands. "Lordy, that was a long time ago. My Lamar and I had just been married two years when we moved here. He worked at the factory, and I had a job as a secretary. I met your mama at the thrift store. She was trying to buy you some baby clothes but was short on money. So I offered her a job and let her clean once every couple of weeks." A faraway look settled in her eyes. "You were just a baby, Macy. She brought you with her."

Macy's mouth tightened. "How was she back then?"

The older woman's eyes lips twitched with a tiny smile. "She was good. Doted on you, she did. Was always stopping and kissing all over you."

"Really?"

"Surely did," Beverly said. "Didn't want to leave you for a second."

Macy inhaled sharply, the pain in that sound tearing at Stone. What had happened to make her mother's behavior change?

"Did she ever mention my father to you?" Macy asked.

Beverly shook her head. "No, and I didn't ask. Didn't figure it was any of my business."

"So you don't know if she had a man in her life or if she was dating anyone?"

"No, all she talked about was you, dear." Beverly set her needles down with a sigh. "Then my Lamar lost his job and took sick, and I had to let her go. I hated it, but I couldn't afford to keep her." She reached out and squeezed Macy's hand. "I'm sorry I can't tell you more. I gave her name to a couple of other folks, though, and they hired her. Then later I heard rumors about how she was acting out, leaving you alone at all times of the night, how she got volatile with Shirley Cregan, and I couldn't believe it. That wasn't the Lynn I knew."

Macy's breath whispered out, anguish riddling it. "Did you talk to them? Did they tell you anything that might have triggered a change in her?"

Beverly shook her head. "I wish I knew. If I had, maybe I could have helped her."

MACY THANKED BEVERLY, a bittersweet feeling flooding her. The Lynn Beverly described was the one she'd seen in those early photographs of the two of them.

So what had happened to turn her into a monster of a mother?

"I know this is hard, Macy," Stone said when they settled into his car. "I can handle the other interviews if you need to take a break."

"Thanks, Stone, but I need to hear what these people have to say. Who's next?"

"Let's talk to the Cregans."

Macy pulled her tablet from the seat. "I'll see

if I can locate the Dansings' phone number while you drive."

Stone turned onto Main Street and drove toward the butcher shop, which was located on the opposite side of the town square. Macy searched DMV records in Charleston and by the time they reached the butcher shop, she had a phone number.

She called the number, and it rang four times, then went to voice mail. She left a message asking them to call her, then hung up just as Stone parked. The butcher shop was in a concrete building that had just gotten a fresh coat of white paint. A middle-aged couple was leaving as they entered, carrying a bag of meat.

For a brief second, Macy wished for that normalcy instead of a life revolving around murder.

The bell over the door tinkled as they entered. A glass-enclosed case faced them, full of various assorted cuts of beef, poultry and pork. A refrigerated case to the side held fresh and frozen meats along with premade meals for easy pickup.

A chunky man with thick silver hair wearing a butcher's apron was working behind the counter while a thin brunette woman in an apron was restocking a basket holding freshly baked bread for sale. The couple looked to be midfifties.

Stone headed to the counter to talk to the man while Macy approached the woman. "Mrs. Cregan? I'm Special Agent Macy Stark."

She nearly dropped a loaf of bread but managed to hang on to it. "I know who you are."

Or course she did. Between the news and the

rumor mill, everyone in town knew she and the sheriff were investigating the mysterious skeletal remains.

"Is there some place we can talk?" Macy glanced at the door, where two men were lumbering in.

"Sure. Troy can handle it out here." She motioned for Macy to follow her into the back, and Stone stepped to the side as the men reached the meat counter. The woman looked at her warily as they settled into chairs in a small office that was cluttered with paperwork.

"I'd like to ask you some questions."

Mrs. Cregan cut her eyes away as if nervous. "I don't know anything about that body, if that's why you're here."

"I understand," Macy said. "My mother disappeared from the psychiatric facility where she was undergoing treatment?"

Mrs. Cregan nodded. "Yes, I heard."

Macy gritted her teeth. "I found my mother's work calendars when I was cleaning out her house," Macy said. "And I saw that she used to clean for you." According to the dates, Macy would have been seven at the time.

"She did for a short while."

"Do you know if she was seeing anyone? Did she ever talk about a man, maybe problems with someone?"

Mrs. Cregan shook her head. "I'm afraid not. But like I said, she just worked for us a short while. Weeks, really."

From her tense tone, Macy detected there had been trouble. "What happened?"

The woman looked down at her hands. "I don't want to talk bad about your mother, Macy."

"Trust me, I haven't worn blinders with her since I was little. I know she had issues. Just tell me what happened."

The woman sighed. "We noticed that she acted erratic sometimes and wasn't always reliable. Showed up sometimes on time and other times didn't show at all. One time the house would be neat and clean, but once it looked as if it had been ransacked."

"That sounds about right. She's bipolar," Macy said.

"Then Troy caught her stealing some of the Hydrocodone he took for his back after he had infusion surgery. We had to let her go then."

Macy took a deep breath. "I'm sorry, Mrs. Cregan. I appreciate your honesty."

The woman squeezed Macy's hand. "I hope you find her and figure out what happened. Things like that can haunt a person."

She had no idea how truly haunted Macy was.

# *Chapter Eleven*

Stone followed Macy to the car, disturbed by the things Troy Cregan had painted of her mother.

Judging from the tight expression on her face, it hadn't gone well with Troy's wife, either. "Macy?"

"She said my mother only worked for them a short time, that she became unreliable. Sometimes cleaned, then sometimes left the house in chaos. They caught her stealing pain meds and let her go." She turned to Stone. "What did Troy say?"

"Do you really want to know?"

Macy crossed her arms. "Stone, I lived with the woman. Nothing you can say is going to surprise me."

He cleared his throat. "He said the same thing, only he wasn't quite so nice about it. Said when he confronted your mother, she became belligerent, picked up a fire poker and swung it at him."

"Good God," Macy said. "Did he report it to the sheriff?"

That would have been Stone's father. "Said he threatened to if she ever came back to their house.

Before she left, though, she overturned furniture and broke lamps."

Macy turned to look back at the butcher shop as he pulled from the drive. "She was lucky they didn't press charges."

Stone's heart squeezed for her. "Let me talk to the others. You don't have to put yourself through this."

"Yes, I do," she said stubbornly. "I can't possibly rest until I know the truth about what happened in that house." She massaged her temple, and he turned onto the side street, then drove to Loretta Pruitt's house. She lived across from the Love 'n Learn Day Care, which she'd run for thirty years but had retired two years ago, and her daughter had taken over the business.

Five minutes later, they knocked on Loretta's door. The plump woman greeted them with the same smile she graced everyone with. She'd never met a stranger and volunteered at the pet rescue shelter, as evidenced by the three cats stretching lazily on the furniture as she invited them in. In the kitchen, she insisted they have a glass of homemade lemonade.

Stone introduced Macy, but Loretta waved off the introduction. "I remember you from when you were little," she said. "Your mother used to clean the day care for me. Brought you along with her. You used to love playing with the blocks and puzzles. Wasn't much into dolls, though."

A tiny smile flitted in Macy's eyes. "That's true. I was more of a tomboy. Into sports."

Loretta fluttered a hand to her chest. "I'm so sorry to hear your mother hasn't been well these last few years."

Macy's expression softened. "Thank you. Most people aren't so kind."

Loretta took Macy's hand. "We're supposed to love our neighbors and help them when they need it."

Macy pursed her lips, her eyes watering. "Thank you again. Can you tell me what you remember about her?"

Loretta sipped her lemonade. "What do you want to know?"

"How was she when she worked for you? And how old was I?"

The woman frowned. "You were about four, if I remember right. Your mama seemed real sweet, a little shy and nervous sometimes, but she took good care of you. At least back then." Her voice cracked. "Later, I heard she left you alone too much. Once when you were about six, I saw her screaming at you in the park. Then she went off and left you."

Stone didn't like the picture he saw in his mind. So far two people described her as loving and kind when Macy was small. But her behavior had become more disturbing, bordering on abusive.

Or *had* it been abusive?

What exactly had gone on behind closed doors?

MACY'S PHONE BUZZED as she and Stone left Loretta's. Pat Dansing's name appeared on the screen, so she answered and put her on Speaker. She didn't want Stone to accuse her of hiding anything.

Stone steered the car in the direction of the cabins on the creek while she explained the reason for her call.

"Yes, I remember your mother," Pat said, her tone cautious.

"She worked for you for a while?" Macy asked.

"Yes, but not for long."

"What happened?" Macy asked. "And please be candid, Mrs. Dansing. She's missing right now, and anything I can learn about her may help find her."

"The truth was that your mother scared my daughter."

Macy's stomach knotted. "What happened?"

"Lucy was five," Pat said. "She was about the same age as you, Macy. We owned the hardware store, and when Ken was out on a buying trip, Lucy would come to the store with me. One day you came in with your mama, and Lucy wanted to play with you, but you touched some of the tools and your mama went crazy. She locked you in the bathroom and started screaming and wouldn't let you out."

Pat hesitated.

"Go on," Macy said.

"Lucy was terrified and crying. Finally, Ken got there, and he unlocked the door and threatened to call DFACS. She dragged you out of there." Her voice trembled. "I...had to calm Lucy down, and Ken told your mother she couldn't come back. But... I...we should have called DFACS right then, but Ken was afraid of what she'd do to retaliate, that she might hurt Lucy." She released a strangled sound. "I've never forgiven myself for not calling and reporting her, though."

Macy swallowed back emotions. "It's not your fault," she said softly. "Social services did come out a few times, but my mother could put on a good act, and they just dismissed it."

The damn system was flawed, Macy thought. Kids got lost in it all the time. Shuffled around from one foster home to another. Sent back to abusive homes where the abuser exercised their anger at being reported on the child.

Thank God for Kate and her mother.

"Mrs. Dansing, did you ever see my mother with a man or hear about her dating someone?"

"No," the woman replied. "After that day, I never talked to her. Truth be told, I avoided her and you. I was too ashamed."

STONE SCRUBBED A hand down his face. They had to keep checking with everyone on the list. Vicki Germaine was next.

But he didn't know how much more he could stand to hear. The picture of Macy as a little girl being abused made him clench the steering wheel in a white-knuckle grip.

Anger churned through him as he maneuvered the switchbacks and climbed the steep incline winding around the mountain. The cabins offered scenic views of the countryside and valley below and private nooks for romantic getaways or families wishing to escape the hustle and bustle of the city.

He turned onto the winding narrow road that led

to the rental office, Macy's silence worrying him. So many of their classmates and their families had fallen apart after the school shooting.

But how had she survived her mother's mental instability and not caved beneath the weight of it and the school massacre?

His admiration for her rose notches.

He parked at the rental office, and Macy climbed out in silence, the weight of what she'd heard today obviously sitting heavily on her shoulders. An SUV was parked in front, but the family came out of the building with keys and left.

Together he and Macy walked up to the entrance and ducked inside. Pamphlets for tourist activities including scenic mountain sights, biking and hiking tours, whitewater rafting and seasonal festivities filled a wall on one side. Maps of the area occupied another and Vicki Germaine, a white-haired lady with bright green eyes stood behind the reception desk.

"Vicki," Stone said in way of greeting. "This is Special Agent Macy Stark."

"I figured you might show up at some point," Vicki said,

Five minutes later, they were seated in a break room with Vicki sipping coffee while a young girl named Tory manned the desk. Stone explained about the investigation, and Macy relayed that she needed to know about her mother when she worked for the rental company.

"That was a long time ago," Vicki said. "But I do remember her."

Stone ground his teeth as Macy asked about Vicki's experience with her mother.

"Lynn Stark was a troubled woman," Vicki said. "She was like two different people. Sometimes she did a good job, and I needed the help, but I had to let her go."

"Why?" Macy asked. "Was she stealing? Doing drugs? Violent?"

Vicki shook her head. "When we had a free room, she used it to bring her lovers there."

Macy's face paled. "Her lovers?"

Vicki nodded. "Don't know any of their names. But one of the handymen walked in on her, and she went off on him. I let her go the next day."

"Is this handyman still around?" Stone asked.

Vicki shook her head. "Passed away last year. Car accident."

"And you had no idea who any of the men were?" Stone asked.

Vicki shook her head. "I never saw them. She always made sure to use a room that wasn't booked and cleaned it so I wouldn't find out."

One of those men could be Macy's father. Or the corpse in the wall in her house.

Stone thanked Vicki, and he and Macy walked back to his car.

"My mother was a piece of work, wasn't she?" Macy muttered as she fastened her seat belt.

Stone made a low sound in his throat. "She was ill," he said. "That doesn't excuse her behavior, but she wasn't in her right mind when she did some of the things she did." Still, Macy had suffered. "It sounds like she loved you as a baby."

Was that enough to make up for the pain and suffering she'd caused Macy the rest of her life?

MACY CLOSED HER EYES, her mind swirling with confusion. If her mother had multiple lovers, maybe she didn't know who had fathered Macy. And any one of them could have come to the house, had an altercation with her mother and ended up dead.

She had a sinking feeling the changes in her mother's behavior had to do with what happened at her house that rainy night.

She struggled to recall her mother mentioning a man, but she'd kept that part of her life private. When she'd asked about her father, her mother had become irate and told her never to ask again.

She hadn't. She'd been too afraid to.

Stone's phone buzzed. "It's the ME," he said, then connected through his hands-free Bluetooth and put it on Speaker. "Sheriff Lawson."

"Sheriff, I know you wanted this ASAP, so I called in a forensic specialist, Dr. Diane Song. She analyzed the bones recovered at the Stark house and confirmed that the body is a male. He was midthirties at the time of death, which was approximately twenty-seven-years ago. I mentioned that he suffered other injuries and ran his DNA in the system."

"Do you have an ID? And why was his name in the system?" Macy asked.

"Because he served time in prison," Dr. Anderson said. "His name is Voight Hubert."

Macy's heart hammered. "What was he in prison for?"

"That's as far as I got. The rest is up to you. I have another body on my table now that I have to get to."

More questions nagged at Macy as they ended the call. Was Hubert the lover her mother had been romantically involved with?

As Stone drove back toward the sheriff's office, she pulled out her tablet. Seconds later, she accessed prison records and found Voight Hubert's name. He had been arrested thirty years ago on felony charges for assault with a deadly weapon and attempted murder.

She pulled up the police report and skimmed it, then found an article about the trial and read it aloud to Stone. Stone pulled into the parking space at his office and cut the engine. Night had fallen, the clouds obliterating the stars tonight and casting a grayness over the town.

"Evidence proved that banker and financial adviser George Billman paid Voight Hubert twenty thousand dollars to kill Billman's wife. Billman was indicted on fraud and conspiracy to commit murder charges. In exchange for his testimony against Billman, Hubert received a lighter sentence."

"Hubert was a hit man?" Stone asked.

"Yes. He was released from prison twenty-eight years ago, so that fits the timeline." Macy chewed the inside of her cheek. "But it makes no sense that he'd tried to hurt my mother. She had no money or enemies that I know of, not anyone who'd hire a hit man to come after her."

"He could have been the man she met at those cabins," Stone suggested.

"I thought of that. But how did he end up dead?"

"Lovers gone awry," Stone said. "It happens a lot. They got in a fight. Things became violent. Physical. He had a record of assault. He could have attacked her."

Macy pursed her lips. "That makes sense, especially with her history." Another disturbing thought occurred to her, and she called Dr. Anderson's number. "It's Special Agent Stark. I need you to do something for me."

"What is it?" Dr. Anderson asked.

Macy inhaled a deep breath. "Run a DNA comparison between Hubert's DNA and mine." If Hubert was her father, she had to know.

# *Chapter Twelve*

Possible scenarios raced through Macy's head.

Lynn Stark could have slept with Hubert years ago, then given birth to Macy. Hubert may or may not have known she was his child. And if he did, he may or may not have wanted to be part of her life.

Her mother could have kept in touch, visited him in prison, or reconnected with him when he was released. If he hadn't known he had a daughter and discovered she was his, he could have been angry with her mother and they'd fought. Or hell, her mother might have been desperate and turned to him for money.

"Macy, do you want to talk?" Stone asked.

She gripped the door handle. "It's been a long day. I just want to turn in."

Indecision played in his eyes. "Are you sure you want to be alone? We could grab dinner."

"Thanks, but I'm going to keep looking through my mother's day planner and see if there's any mention of Hubert."

"All right. Call me, though, if you change your mind."

She murmured she would, then climbed out and walked to her car. On the way back to the inn, she picked up a sandwich at the diner, then carried it to her room. Her classmates who'd stayed at the inn during the reunion were gone now, and families and couples occupied the space, their chatter and laughter a reminder that she had no family of her own.

Stone's invitation to dinner taunted her. He was strong, handsome, a hero in town. An alpha man with heart and soul. The kind of man a woman could count on.

But she'd allowed herself to lean on Trey Cushing when she'd been vulnerable, and that had been a huge mistake.

She and Trey never should have gotten married. But she'd been hurting and traumatized and vulnerable after the shooting, and Trey had offered a strong shoulder to cry on. He'd also been charming.

But that charm disappeared after they were married, and he'd become controlling. He also had anger issues that emerged when she stood up to him. Within months, she'd known she had to get out of the marriage.

But an unexpected pregnancy had made her try to work it out.

Trey hadn't wanted a family, though, and asked her to make it go away.

She knew what it was like to grow up unloved and refused his demands. Had vowed to raise the child alone and make certain her baby felt wanted and loved every single day of his or her life.

Anguish tightened her chest. But at seven weeks, she'd had a miscarriage.

Trey had been relieved. She was devastated. But it was the catalyst she needed to make the split.

Stone was nothing like Trey. But she couldn't get involved with him now. Not when her life was such a mess.

STONE COULDN'T TAKE his mind off Macy's troubled childhood. She had all the reason in the world to be bitter or have a chip on her shoulder, but she'd made something of herself and used the trauma of her past to help shape her into a good, caring citizen.

His own childhood seemed cushy compared to hers.

He shouldn't have been surprised that she'd requested a DNA comparison to Hubert. He should have thought of it himself.

How would she feel if she learned her father was an ex-con?

The streetlights illuminated the cars and people out wandering the stores and enjoying dining out. His deputy was back at the station, so he could take a break. The new coffee shop, the Grind, sat on the corner across from Daisy's Diner and was overflowing now that it offered wine, beer and specialty after-dinner drinks and desserts.

He was tempted to stop for a beer but decided to go home instead, just in case Macy changed her mind and wanted company. But just as he turned onto the street leading to his house, a call came in.

"Sheriff," his deputy said when Stone responded.

"Got a call from Blues & Brews. Bar brawl just broke out. I'm on my way there now." Tension stretched over the line for a minute. "Your brother is involved."

Dammit. "I'll be right there." Stone spun the squad car around, flipped on the siren, then sped toward the pub. Blues & Brews was at the edge of town and offered bar food, drinks and live music. Tonight was open mic night. He'd encouraged Mickey to play and sing one night, but his brother had shut down and left in a huff.

The neon lights of the giant beer mug boasting the name of the bar shone bright against the dark sky. The parking lot was full, so he swung into a space across the street. Blues music flowed from the speakers and bled outside, the hammering of boots pounding the floor indicating the dance floor had opened up.

Just as he approached, the door opened and two men tumbled out the door, swinging fists and rolling across the ground. Stone cursed and jogged over to the scene. A few patrons had stepped outside, gawking, while two brawny men were trying to break it up.

He saw Mickey throw a punch and miss, his voice slurred as he yelled. The two of them fell to the ground together, grinding into the gravel as they traded blows. He quickly scanned them both in search of weapons and was relieved when he didn't spot a gun or knife.

"Get back!" he shouted at the spectators, then strode to the men and shouted at them to stop.

Mickey bellowed at him, but Stone grabbed his

arm to pull him off the other man. His deputy arrived then and yanked the other man to his feet. He was staggering and swaying, mumbling obscenities.

Mickey jerked at Stone. "Let me go!"

"Not until you settle down, little brother," Stone said, well aware that everyone was watching.

"Give it up, man," his deputy growled at the drunk.

Stone addressed the growing crowd of spectators, "Show's over, folks. Go on back inside." He glanced at the bartender. "What happened?"

He gestured toward the man Mickey had been fighting. "I don't know. One minute they were talking football, the next shouting and throwing fists."

Stone thanked him, then motioned for him to go inside. "We've got it. Sorry about this. If there are damages inside, let me know."

"Thanks, Sheriff." The bartender nodded, then ducked back inside.

"Take him home," he told Murphy. "I'll drive Mickey home myself."

The crowd dispersed, Murphy hauled the drunk toward his police car, and Stone yanked at his brother's arm.

"Go away," Mickey muttered.

Stone steeled his jaw to control his anger and dragged Mickey across the street to his car. He yanked open the door and pushed his brother inside.

"I can take care of myself," Mickey mumbled, his voice slurred.

"To hell you can. Just get in and shut up," Stone growled.

He slammed the door, then got inside and headed toward Mickey's. Something had to change. His brother needed help.

BEFORE MACY TACKLED looking through the remaining day planners, she decided to call the Walkmans. They were the only ones from her initial list that she hadn't spoken with. Their personal number wasn't available to the public, but she finally got the number for Mr. Walkman's administrative assistant, a man named Ryan Barkin.

"Mr. Barkin, I'm trying to reach the Walkmans, either Mrs. Walkman or Mr. Walkman. I need one of them to call me back ASAP."

"What is this about?" Barkin asked.

"I'm investigating the death of a man who was found dead at my mother Lynn Stark's house in Briar Ridge. I'm talking to everyone who knew her at the time. She cleaned houses for the Walkmans, so I just have some basic questions to ask them about her state of mind when she worked for them."

"I see," Barkin said. "The Walkmans have a busy schedule with the campaign, but I'll relay the message."

Macy thanked him, then hung up and turned back to the calendars. She spent the next two hours scouring the calendars and made a second list consisting of five more names and calling them. Two were single women who both stated they felt sorry for Lynn but couldn't handle her mood swings. One couple used to own an antique store and admitted that Macy's mother broke several items in the store and appeared to be intoxicated or on drugs, so they fired her.

Another man, whose wife had died of heart failure, had dementia himself and was now in a nursing home, so she dismissed him as not being able to help.

Frustrated, she decided to look into the social worker who'd visited the house. She put in a call to find her name but with the late hour, had to leave a message.

Next, she dug deeper into Hubert. She found records indicating he'd been in juvie, but the records were sealed. Another assault charge had been placed but withdrawn by the female who'd reported a break-in at her house.

She scratched her head wondering why the woman had dropped the charges. Maybe a domestic situation? Women often recanted charges out of fear or because they were involved with the assailant and softened, then took him back. Others knew the arrest would only trigger more violence and backed out, blaming themselves and opting to remain in an abusive relationship.

She searched for the woman's name and found it listed as Angie Wickins. A quick background check revealed that she owned a gardening shop outside Briar Ridge.

Macy made a mental note to talk to her tomorrow. She'd also call the prison where Hubert had been incarcerated and find out his cellmate's name. After twenty-seven years it was a long shot, but she had to pursue every angle.

Exhausted, she tucked the files away, dragged on a tank top and cotton pajama pants and crawled in bed. The lavender color was soothing and spa-like, the flowers on the table wafting sweetness and summer.

Yet when she closed her eyes, the beauty faded and all she saw was the dark dungeon-like basement at her mother's and Hubert's bony hand protruding through the broken plaster.

Her phone buzzed, and she snagged it from the nightstand and checked the number, expecting Stone or maybe the Walkmans. But the screen read unknown.

Clenching the phone with a shaky hand, she pressed Connect.

A muffled voice spoke. "Stop asking questions or you'll end up dead, too."

"MICKEY, YOU'RE KILLING YOURSELF with this binge drinking," Stone said as he escorted his brother inside his house. "You have to stop."

"What do you care?" Mickey snarled as she staggered to the sofa and dropped down onto it.

How could he get through to his brother? "Of course I care. You're all I've got."

"I don't need you," Mickey said, then closed his eyes and laid his hand over his face with a groan.

"Maybe not. But you need a program," Stone said. "There's an AA group that meets at the church on Wednesdays. If you want, I'll go with you."

"I'm not going to go listen to a bunch of whiners," Mickey said. "I'm not like them."

But he was. “Maybe not,” Stone said. “But they could help you figure out why you drink so much. Why you’re throwing away your life like this.”

“I know you like to play hero, but I don’t need you to rescue me.”

“You resent me because I should have taken that bullet instead of you,” Stone said. “I wish it had been me. I’ll never forgive myself for not stopping what happened.”

“There you go, thinking you’re supposed to save everyone,” Mickey said, his words slurring. “But you can’t. You can’t save me…”

A knot of fear tightened Stone’s belly. “I’m not giving up on you, little brother. I’m not.”

Angry and frustrated, he strode outside before his temper got the best of him. He’d wait until Mickey was sober, then he’d try again.

His phone buzzed as he got in his car. Macy. Pulse jumping, he answered.

“Someone just called and threatened me,” Macy said.

Stone’s breath caught. “Male or female?”

“I couldn’t tell,” Macy said. “The voice was muffled. But it was a warning—stop asking questions or I’d end up dead.”

Stone muttered a curse. “I’ll be right over.”

“I’m fine, Stone,” Macy said. “I’ve already called to put a trace on my phone. If the caller phones back, maybe we can trace the call.”

“To be on the safe side, I want to be able to track your phone, too,” Stone said. “Is that okay?”

“I guess that would be smart,” Macy agreed, although she sounded reluctant. Her pride be damned. Her safety was more important.

"Where are you?" Stone asked.

"At the inn. Don't worry, I'm inside for the night."

Stone glanced back at his brother's house. He was worried to death about Mickey and hated to leave him. And now Macy… He wanted to go to her and hold her in his arms. To make sure she stayed safe all night.

But she'd built walls around herself just like Mickey. And just like he had years ago.

He was already losing Mickey.

He couldn't stand to care too much about anyone else and then lose them, too.

THE NEXT MORNING, Macy met Stone at the station, explained about Angie Wickins, and he drove them to the gardening center where Angie was employed. He looked a little rough around the edges, as if he hadn't slept much. Neither had she.

"Are you all right?" Macy asked as he wound up the mountain.

Stone's dark gaze met hers, emotions flickering for a second before he wiped them off his face and maneuvered another turn. "Fine. Did you hear about the trace?"

"Came from a burner phone, just as I expected," Macy said.

"Figures. Someone knew those are almost impossible to trace," Stone said.

A thick silence fell between them as he drove, the case weighing on Macy. Her mother's face had taunted her all night. She thought she'd seen her outside the window. Saw her running through the woods behind her house, a bloody knife in her hand.

The sun was struggling to break though the storm clouds but failing, and gray streaked the sky, adding a dreariness to the day and making her want to crawl back in bed and bury herself beneath the covers.

For a split second, she closed her eyes and imagined she wasn't alone in the world—or in that bed. That Stone had crawled in beside her and was holding her tight. She felt safe and cared for and her heart pounded as he touched her cheek, then pressed his lips against hers.

They hit a pothole, jarring her back to the present, and Stone veered up the graveled drive to the gardening center. Several pickup trucks and SUVs sat in the parking lot, customers already filling the cabs and trunks with assorted plants and flowers.

The bright red, purple, yellow and pink perennials dotted the landscape with color. Marigolds and sunflowers drew her eye with their cheery blooms.

Together she and Stone walked up to the front of the store, which held potting supplies, ceramic pots, bird feeders and other essentials. Two workers strolled through the outside area where customers combed the aisles.

A fortysomething auburn-haired woman wearing a gardening apron was working the register, her name tag reading Angie. Her hair was piled on top of her head in a messy knot, and dirt stained her apron as if she lived and breathed her work.

She and Stone exchanged a look as they approached the counter. Her eyes widened in recognition when she saw them, then confusion flashed across her slender face.

"Can we talk in private?" Stone asked.

She nodded, as if she didn't want to discuss whatever they'd come to talk to her about in front of her customers. Then she waved a young twentysomething girl over. "Rachel, can you work the register?"

"Sure." Rachel left the stack of birdseed she'd been arranging for sale and sauntered over, smiling as she took Angie's place at the register. Angie motioned for them to follow her through the back section to a small office and closed the door.

She fidgeted with her hands, then picked up a packet of flower seed and tapped it in her palm. "What is this about?"

"Have you seen the news about a body being found in a house in Briar Ridge?"

The seeds rattled as Angie continued to tap them. "I saw it. But what's that got to do with me?"

Macy licked her dry lips. "We identified the dead man as Voight Hubert," Macy said.

Angie gasped, surprise flitting across her face.

"I don't know anything about that," she said, her voice cracking.

Macy's instincts surged to life. "But you did know Voight Hubert, didn't you?"

She stiffened, working her mouth from side to side. "Why are you asking?"

Stone cleared his throat. "Because we know that

he was arrested for assaulting you, and that you dropped the charges."

Angie closed her eyes for a second as if to stem her emotions. Or perhaps to give herself time to concoct a lie.

Macy softened her tone. "Angie, this is obviously painful for you to discuss. But I need to know what happened. Did he assault you?"

She gave a tiny nod of her head. "But I don't want that to come out again. It was hard enough the first time."

"How old were you?" Macy asked.

"Eighteen," Angie said. "I was at a club with some friends and didn't notice that he was watching me. I went out to my car to leave and he cornered me. He grabbed me and dragged me into the woods…" Her voice broke, and Macy squeezed her hand.

"Take your time," Macy murmured.

"I screamed and fought him," Angie said. "I even bit his hand, but he was strong and drunk and…"

"He raped you?" Macy asked.

She shook her head and fidgeted with her hands. "He was going to, but this other guy in the parking lot heard me scream and came running. He knocked the creep off of me and punched him, then called 911."

"A Good Samaritan," Stone said.

"Sure was." Angie nodded with a tiny smile. "I ended up marrying him."

Macy smiled. "Is he here now?"

Sadness flickered in her eyes. "I lost him three years ago to a drunk driver," Angie said. "He and I took this place over when my daddy retired. Every time I plant seeds or see the flowers blooming, I think of him."

Macy's heart squeezed at the love in her tone. "Why did you drop the charges?" she asked.

Angie cut her eyes away. "My father. He flew into a rage and said everyone would blame me because I was underage and had a beer. It was so stupid of me..."

"It was not your fault," Macy said.

"But what he said was true. People would have talked, gossiped," Angie said, a wary acceptance in her voice. "Stared at me."

Macy understood about that. Sexual assault victims were often treated like criminals themselves. No wonder so many didn't follow through in court.

"Anyway, Daddy said he wanted to protect me, that they'd make me out to be a tramp. And I just wanted it to go away," Angie said. "So I agreed." She cut her eyes away again, and Macy sensed she was holding back.

Macy rubbed her arm. "What aren't you telling us? *Did* Hubert just go away?"

"He actually showed up at my house one night about a month after that, was outside watching me through the window. My father caught him and threatened to kill him if he ever came near me again."

# *Chapter Thirteen*

Stone balled his hands into fists. He'd heard similar stories before, but they enraged him every time. His father had taught him to respect women. To protect them. "What happened after that? Did Hubert ever come back?"

"I never saw him," Angie said. "And my father and I never spoke of it again."

Stone's breath eased out. "Where is your father now? We'd like to talk to him."

"That's impossible," Angie said. "He died ten years ago."

"Angie," Macy said. "Do you think your father would have made good on that threat?"

The woman wiped her hands on her jeans. "I don't know. Why? Are you trying to say he killed that vile man who attacked me?"

"I don't know what to think." Macy softened her tone. "What about the man you married?"

"What about him?" Angie's voice turned defensive.

"Did he ever talk to Hubert?" Stone asked.

"You're not pinning that vile man's death on my

daddy or on my sweet husband." Angie stood. "I've said too much already. I have to get back to work."

Her posture rigid, she gestured for them to leave her office.

Macy pushed a card into her hand. "If you think of something else, please call me."

Angie stuffed the card into her pocket and gave Macy a dark look.

Stone followed Angie back through the gardening shop. He and Macy waited until they'd settled in his car before he spoke.

"Interesting story. If Angie's father or husband had anything to do with Hubert's death, she obviously doesn't intend to tell us."

"No, she's protective of them." Macy buckled her seat belt. "Considering what happened, I can't say as I blame her. After all this time, with both men deceased, it'll be hard to prove their involvement."

"And if one of them murdered Hubert, how did he end up in your house?"

"Good question."

Stone's mind raced. "Do you remember if your mother ever went to that gardening center? Maybe she had a delivery or gardener come out to tend the yard?"

Macy pinched the bridge of her nose as if struggling to recall. "I don't remember her gardening as I got older, but she may have when I was young. When I was looking at old pictures, there was a flower garden out front. But she must have let it all die later on after her break. And she never hired anyone to help. We didn't have the money." She angled her head to look at Stone. "What are you thinking?"

"Just looking at every possibility," Stone said. "Both Angie's father and her husband had reason to hate Hubert."

"True, but they work in the gardening business," Macy said. "Why wouldn't they have just buried him somewhere? That would have been easier than putting him in a wall where he might be found."

Stone considered that. "That makes sense." Only it put them back to square one.

MACY CONTEMPLATED OTHER possibilities as Stone started the engine. If Angie's father or husband knew her mother was unstable, they could have decided she'd make a good scapegoat if the body was ever discovered. After all, who would believe a psychotic woman?

If that was the case, what if her mother came home and found them or the body, and that triggered her break?

*You're grasping at straws. Trying to justify any way you can that she was not at fault or directly connected to the man's brutal murder.*

Stone drove back toward town, and Macy's stomach knotted when she spotted Gretta's BMW parked in front of the station.

"The vulture's here," Stone muttered.

"I guess being a predator is a necessary evil to do her job."

A wry smile curved his mouth. "I'll handle her if you want to hide out in my office."

Macy shook her head. "I can't run from it," she said. "I tried that before, yet here I am now."

Stone squeezed her hand, and they got out and walked into the station. Gretta was talking to Deputy Bridges when they entered, a flirtatious gleam in her eyes as she leaned close to him.

Macy rolled her eyes. The woman could be charming—when she wanted something. Maybe the deputy had fallen for it and was feeding her information.

Gretta straightened when she saw them and gestured toward her sidekick, a cameraman named Rickey. "Sheriff Lawson, Special Agent Stark, do you have an update on the investigation into the homicide?"

Stone squared his shoulders. "We have identified the man as an ex-con named Voight Hubert who served time in prison for being a hired hit man. At this point, we don't know how he ended up at the Stark house. He was killed approximately twenty-seven years ago. Anyone with information about him should please call the sheriff's office."

Gretta pushed the mic toward Macy. "Special Agent Stark, any word on your mother who escaped the psychiatric hospital?"

Macy's lungs tightened. Gretta seemed to take pleasure in pointing out her mother's mental illness. "No word at this time. Again, we're asking anyone who sees or speaks to her to report it to the police."

Gretta narrowed her eyes, scrutinizing Macy. "Do you think that your mother is dangerous?"

Macy swallowed hard. Did she? "We have no

reason to believe that at this time, but she is wanted for questioning."

"But you grew up with her, Agent Stark," Gretta said sharply. "Did she exhibit violent behavior when you were a child?"

Macy struggled not to react, but Stone stepped in. "We are not here to speculate, but to find facts. Agent Stark's personal relationship with her mother is not up for comment."

Stone took Macy's arm and ushered her back toward his office. "That woman," he growled.

Macy blinked back unwanted tears. "She's just doing her job."

"Don't defend her. She enjoys putting people on the spot," Stone said, his tone angry. He paced to his desk and looked out the window. "I think Bridges is leaking her information. If I find out that's true, I'm going to have his head on a platter."

Macy moved to the table in the corner and pulled her laptop from her shoulder bag, and Stone went to grab coffee. Her phone buzzed, and the name Walkman appeared on her screen. She answered the call and introduced herself.

"This is Adeline Walkman," the woman said. "I was asked to call you. I just saw the news about your mother and that man's murder."

"Yes," Macy said. "I understand that Lynn Stark cleaned house for you at one time."

"That's true," Mrs. Walkman said, a note of sympathy to her voice. "But that was years ago, and we haven't had any contact with her since. I'm sorry to hear she's been in a psychiatric hospital."

Macy swallowed to tamp down an emotional response. "Thank you so much, Mrs. Walkman."

"Please call me Adeline. Now, how can I help?"

"I'm looking for any information you can give me about her."

"Well, it's been a long time, and she only worked for us a couple of months. We lost our son to an accident and decided to move. Too many painful memories in Briar Ridge."

"I understand that, and I'm so sorry for your loss," Macy said. More than the woman knew. "Did she happen to ever mention having a boyfriend?"

A heartbeat passed. "I'm afraid not. We didn't discuss personal things at all. I was working for a nonprofit back then, so she usually came to clean when I was out of the house. I left a check for her, and she was gone when I returned home."

Macy exhaled. "Thanks for returning my call. If you think of anything else, please let me know."

"I will. And I hope you find her and get her the help she needs."

Macy thanked her again, hung up and turned back to her laptop just as Stone loped in with two cups of coffee.

"Thanks," she said as she took the cup. "Just talked to Adeline Walkman. That was a dead end."

"Sorry, Macy," Stone said.

Macy shrugged. "It was a long shot. It's not like Mother had any real friends she'd confide in. "I'm going to look into Hubert more," she said. "See if he had family or if anyone reported him missing."

She spent the next half hour checking missing

persons reports while Stone called the prison where Hubert had been incarcerated to inquire about his cellmates.

"No one reported Hubert missing," Macy said. "Did he have family?"

"Let me check." Next, she ran a search into Hubert's past in search of relatives. "No surviving family members, and he never married. His mother was a cocaine addict. Voight was removed from her custody and placed in foster care at age three, where he was tossed around from one home to another."

So he wasn't close enough to anyone that they would have missed him.

STONE TOOK A long sip of his coffee. "Warden said Hubert had two cellmates. Man in for beating his kid to death with a baseball bat. Died in a prison fight a few months after Hubert was incarcerated."

"Sounds like he got what he deserved," Macy said.

Stone nodded. "Second cellmate was a man named Bubba Yates. Did time for a hit-and-run. Downed a half pint of whiskey, then got behind the wheel." At least with Mickey's loss of sight, he couldn't drive. Stone had always hated that loss of independence for his brother. At the moment though, he was glad he couldn't get behind the wheel and hurt himself or anyone else. "Served seven years for vehicular manslaughter."

Macy plugged the man's name into her laptop and ran a search. "Looks like he lives outside Hendersonville. Let's go talk to him."

Stone grabbed his keys. "We'll grab lunch on the way." Stone told Murphy where he was going as they left the station.

The temperature outside was climbing to the eighties, but a slight breeze stirred the trees and gave some relief. They stopped for barbecue sandwiches, then Stone wound through the mountains, the heart of the apple houses where people flocked in the fall to pick apples and purchase homemade apple jellies, pies, breads and apple butter.

Macy searched for more information on Yates and learned he worked at a hardware store. She called the owner, who relayed that he was at work, so they drove straight to the store.

The sun was beaming down hotter as they parked and went inside. Stone identified himself to the clerk and asked for Yates. He was a rail-thin man wearing a shirt emblazoned with the hardware store's name.

Stone asked him to step outside with them, and the man's look turned wary.

"Am I in trouble or something?" Yates asked.

Stone shook his head, then explained they wanted to talk about Hubert.

"That's a name from the past." Yates pulled something from his pocket and rolled it around in his palm. "I haven't seen or talked to him since I got out of prison."

"You never reconnected when he was released?"

"No way." He opened his palm to reveal a sobriety chip. "I found God in prison, joined AA and been sober ever since." A sadness tinged his eyes.

"Don't change what I did, though. Have to live with that guilt every day."

Stone understood about guilt.

"Mr. Yates, Hubert's body was recently found in Briar Ridge," Macy said. "He's been there for twenty-seven years."

Yates's brows shot up. "I swear I never talked to him or saw him after I got out. He was trouble, and I didn't want anything to do with him."

"We understand that he served time for taking money to kill a woman," Stone said. "Did he talk about that?"

"Just that he was sorry he got caught. I'm telling you, he was a mean one."

"Did he have any visitors that you remember?" Macy asked.

The man ran his thin hand over a scar on his cheek. Stone wondered if he'd gotten it in the accident or in prison. "Heard him talking to another inmate about some woman visiting him. But he never mentioned her name, and I didn't ask."

"Was it a romantic visit? Someone he knew?" Macy asked.

Yates shrugged. "Don't think so. Said he was going to get a big payday when he was released."

Stone glanced at Macy. Sounded like he might have been planning another job. Who had he been hired to kill?

WHILE STONE DROVE them back to the station, Macy called the prison warden and identified herself. "We spoke with a former cellmate of Voight Hubert. He said Hubert had a visit from a female before his release. Can you look back at the visitor logs and find out who she was?"

A long second passed. "That was a long time ago."

"It's important," Macy said impatiently. "We're trying to solve a murder."

"Why the big rush? It's been over two decades," he said.

Macy tightened her fingers around the phone. "Two reasons. One, the man's body was found in my own house. And we have reason to believe that visitor may have hired Hubert to kill someone else. That happened on your watch."

The man cursed. "All right, but it'll take some time. We weren't digitized back then, so logs will be archived. I'll get my assistant to see if she can dig up those records."

"Do you have security footage of the visitors where we might get a look at her?"

"I'll see what I can find."

"Check his mail, too, for anything suspicious. And see if anyone put money into his account while he was there."

"If a piece of mail was suspicious, we would have reported it. Otherwise after all this time, it would have been discarded," he said. "But I'll see if there's a record of anything suspicious filed and look into his account. I'll get back to you ASAP."

BACK AT THE SHERIFF'S OFFICE, Stone looked up as his deputy poked his head in. "Sheriff, a call just came in. Neighbor was driving by the old Simmons place and thought she saw someone breaking in. I'll check it out."

Stone stood. "Agent Stark and I will go. I want you to look around at any abandoned properties or rentals not being used, in case Lynn Stark is hiding out in one of them."

Murphy gave a nod. "Copy that."

Macy gathered her laptop and shoulder bag. "Let's go."

Dusk was falling by the time they reached the Simmons place, an old farm with chicken houses that had fallen into disrepair years before.

"Do you recall Martha and Tim Simmons?" Stone asked.

"Yes," Macy said. "Their daughter ran track with me."

"They moved after the shooting," Stone said. "Couldn't sell the place. Farm went into foreclosure."

"No one wanted to move to the town where kids got slaughtered," Macy said.

Stone nodded grimly. "Thankfully that's changing now with the new school in the fall."

"Kate was pretty amazing," Macy said, her voice filled with affection and a tinge of sadness. "I never would have survived growing up without her and her mother."

Stone laid his hand over hers. "I'm glad you had her, Macy. And sorry we weren't friends back then."

"I wasn't exactly the social type," Macy said.

And now he understood the reason.

Storm clouds moved across the sky, painting the

mountains a gloomy gray. In the distance, he could see it raining on top of Bear Mountain, the trees shivering with the wind. He and Macy scanned the property as he maneuvered the narrow graveled drive.

There were no cars in sight.

If Macy's mother was here, how had she gotten this far? Had she stolen another vehicle and ditched it? Or maybe she hitchhiked?

"It looks sad and run-down," Macy said.

"A lot of properties around here do," Stone said. "But it could be revitalized if someone ever wanted to buy it and turn it back into a working farm."

He slowed as he approached the white farmhouse and glanced at the ripped screens and peeling paint, then to the right where two chicken houses were abandoned. A rotting barn was missing a roof.

He parked, and Macy climbed from the vehicle and quietly closed the door, her face strained with anxiety. Still, she was focused.

Together they started up the drive but suddenly a noise to the right jerked his attention to the window, and then a gunshot rang out.

Macy ducked behind an oak tree, and he darted beside her, both pulling their guns. He pivoted to the left and she went right, visually sweeping the property to see where the shot had come from.

# *Chapter Fourteen*

Macy gripped her gun at the ready and peered around the edge of the tree in search of the shooter. Another shot rang out, whizzing past her, and Stone motioned that he'd spotted someone at the window. The screen was torn, the glass broken, and a shotgun poked through the hole.

"Police, put down the gun!" he shouted.

"Mom, are you in there?" Macy yelled. "If you are, drop the gun and let's talk."

The barrel of the gun bobbed, but the door remained shut.

"Open up and put the gun on the porch!" Stone shouted. "No one has to get hurt. We just want to talk."

Macy eased along the bushes, taking cover, and he picked up a rock and threw it against the woodpile to create a distraction. She ran for the back of the house and crept up the steps to the back door. Inching slowly, she kept her eyes peeled in case the shooter realized she was coming in from the back.

The wind whistled through the trees in the back, the rotting boards of the back stoop creaking. She eased open the screen door, sweeping the interior as she tiptoed inside. The house was dark and smelled of must and mold. Except for a rickety pine table, the outdated kitchen looked empty, floral wallpaper peeling from the dingy walls.

She eased through the room into a hallway, then spotted the living room, which held a dusty-looking plaid sofa and a coffee table that listed to one side from a broken leg.

She plastered herself against the wall and peered into the room from the door and saw a hunched figure at the window holding the shotgun.

A man, not her mother.

"Lower the gun and step away," Macy said firmly.

At the sound of her voice, he swung around, the shotgun waving in his shaky hands. His eyes looked crazed as if he was high, and he swayed. She guessed his age to be midsixties. An empty liquor bottle sat on an end table with several bottles of pills.

"Please put the gun down," Macy said softly. "I don't want anyone to get hurt."

He looked confused when he glanced down at the gun, as if he didn't know what he was doing. She inched closer to him, holding up her hand to indicate she wasn't going to shoot.

The weapon bobbed up and down, but he slowly lowered it to his side. "I ain't done nothing wrong," he said, his words slurring.

"Then you don't have anything to worry about,"

Macy said. "I came here looking for my mother. I thought she was in here."

"Ain't nobody here but me."

"What's your name, sir?" Macy asked.

"Floyd. Floyd Gleason," he muttered.

"Listen Floyd. So far you haven't done anything wrong. I'm sure you fired that shot to protect yourself," she said in a soothing tone. "But if you shoot again or don't give up the gun, I'm going to have to arrest you."

His expression was confused as he looked up at her, and she gave him a nod of encouragement. "Please. Just lower it."

He slowly laid the gun on the floor, and she shouted at Stone to come in. He entered cautiously, taking in the scene.

"What are you doing here?" Stone asked.

"Just sleeping," the older man said. "Wasn't hurting anyone. Ain't nobody lived here in forever."

Stone checked the pills on the table. "Oxy."

"For my back," the man said. "Got so much pain I can hardly walk."

"Do you have any family we can call?" Macy asked.

Emotions streaked the man's face, and he shook his head.

Sympathy for him welled inside Macy. This man didn't pose a threat. He was just homeless and lonely. "Let us take you to a shelter," Macy said. "You can get some help there, a hot meal and a bed."

"Just let me be," the man said.

Stone stepped forward. "Come on, I know a place where you can go and be with some friends."

The man reluctantly agreed, and Macy took his weapon while Stone helped him to the car.

Thirty minutes later, they dropped him at a group home for men run by the preacher at the community church. Stone looked troubled as they left.

"Let's call it a night," he said when they reached the station. "I need to check on my brother."

"Is he okay?" Macy asked.

Stone shrugged. "Not really."

Macy's phone buzzed with a text from the ME.

DNA from Hubert is not a familial match to yours.

A sliver of relief flitted through Macy. At least her birth father wasn't a hired killer.

But if Hubert wasn't her father, then who was? And why had Hubert been at her mother's house?

STONE COULDN'T SHAKE his nagging worry about Mickey. If his brother didn't get some help, he might end up like the man he'd just dropped at the group home.

He left Macy at her car, drove by and picked up burgers, then headed to Mickey's. When he arrived, he noticed the house looked dark. He started to leave but knew he wouldn't sleep unless he saw his brother, so he grabbed the bag of food and carried it to the door.

He knocked, then twisted the doorknob. "Mickey, are you here?"

No answer. "Mickey!" he called as he strode into the living room. "Hey, man, I brought burgers." He dropped them on the kitchen counter, then strode to Mickey's office, hoping to find him at work. The desk was a mess, his laptop was open, but Mickey wasn't inside the room.

He went to the bedroom next and glanced inside. Dammit, his brother was piled in the bed, snoring. A half dozen beer cans sat on the dresser, an open one on his nightstand. Stone crossed to the bed and nudged him.

"Mickey, wake up, man. Eat something."

Mickey grunted and pulled the covers over his head.

"Come on, little brother. We have to talk."

"Go away," Mickey growled.

"I'm trying to help you. If you don't get your act together, you're going to lose your job."

"I already did," Mickey said. "Now get out."

Frustration filled Stone. "I'll leave, but I'm going to make a pot of coffee. There are burgers on the counter."

His heart heavy, Stone turned and strode from the room. He sat for a half hour watching the house, hoping Mickey would turn the lights on and get up. But the house remained dark, and he saw no movement inside.

Another half hour, and a helpless feeling engulfed him as he drove away.

MACY DECIDED TO search her mother's house again, this time focusing on something that might lead her to her father or a connection to Hubert.

Just as she parked, though, the warden called. "The name on the visitor log was Nellie Norris," he said. "Sorry, but I couldn't find a photo or video of the visit. The archived records room is a mess. Had some flooding a few years back, so some of them might have been thrown out if they were damaged."

Macy sighed. "I appreciate you looking," she said. "I'll see what I can find on Nellie Norris."

Macy thanked him again and hung up. Then, anxious for information, she pulled her laptop from her bag, booted it up and ran a search for the woman. First, she checked DMV records and found two women by that name. The first lived in Raleigh and was twenty, so her age didn't fit. The second was a thirty-five-year-old, which also didn't fit. Twenty-seven years ago, she would have been eight.

She deepened the search and found another Nellie Norris who died at the age of eighty the year before. It was possible she could have been the woman who'd visited Hubert, but if so, she would be no help now.

If her mother had visited him, her age didn't fit with any of these women, either.

A dead end.

Or was it possible that the woman had faked her identity to see Hubert? There were security measures in place to prevent that from happening, but a smart person with connections could find a way to circumvent them.

Gritting her teeth, she shut down her laptop and stowed it back in her bag.

Thunder rumbled, the storm clouds gathering on the horizon threatening rain. She opened the car door and hurried up to the house before the downpour started. The crime scene tape flapped in the wind. Her hand trembled as she entered, the musty odor mingling with the scent of her own fear.

Whispers of evil echoed through the eaves of the old house, and the thin walls shook as the rain outside began. Memories of hiding in the closet bombarded her, her mother's erratic screams drifting to her from the place in her mind where she thought she'd locked them away forever. She pictured her mother in the kitchen in a thin cotton gown, her hands shaking as she lifted a water glass to her lips and took a sip, washing down a handful of pills.

Another memory surfaced—country music played on an ancient radio, her mother taking her hands and dancing in the kitchen, singing and swirling Macy around in a dizzying rhythm. A smile tilted her mouth. She'd forgotten that occasionally she had a pleasant moment or two. The painful memories seemed to have washed away those times like a heavy rain crushing the pansies her mother had planted during one of her good days.

Pulling herself from the memory, she decided to check the hall closet. A couple of her mother's old coats were still inside, so she checked the pockets and found a few receipts from the drugstore, a gum wrapper and some loose change. A pair of rain boots sat on the floor, and a shoebox was on the top shelf. She brought it down and looked inside. Folders with assorted bills, then several old checkbooks and statements were inside.

A streak of lightning zigzagged across the sky,

illuminating the foggy window, and took her back to that horrible night when the storm woke her.

*A tree branch scraped the window, clawing at it like sharp fingernails. The limbs looked like giant hands reaching for her. Glass rattled, then shattered and rain blew in, the wind roaring like an animal.*

*She screamed and dragged the covers up to hide, but the floor creaked and she suddenly smelled a musky odor. Clenching the covers in her hands, she peeked and saw a shadow looming above her bed.*

*She screamed, thunder drowning out the sound, then she heard footsteps and her door squeaking open, then closing. Shaking in terror, she slid from beneath the covers, then crawled under the bed and covered her mouth with her hand. She lay still, afraid to move, afraid the man would return and get her, but she kept her eyes peeled toward the door.*

*Seconds ticked by. The rain beat down. The lightning popped.*

*Then she heard the noise in the hall. Footsteps. Something banging. Her mother screaming...*

Macy gripped the wall to steady herself as the memory slowly blurred and reality returned. Thunder boomed outside, sending a shudder coursing through her. Suddenly the monsters were everywhere in the house, shadowy figures floating through the walls, darting across the ceiling, eyes piercing her.

She didn't want to spend another minute in this house. Not tonight.

Heart hammering, she rushed to the door, ran

outside to her car and stored the box in the back seat. Brush crackled behind her and she spun around and thought she saw someone move, going into the house.

Was it her mother?

Exhaling a shaky breath, she jogged back to the house, raindrops splattering her. If her mother was inside, she'd make her talk.

She paused at the doorway, then crept forward and peered inside. "Mom?"

The floor creaked and she pivoted, but suddenly something hard slammed against the side of her head. Macy staggered and grabbed at the wall, then her attacker's arm. But the room spun and stars danced behind her eyes.

She blinked, struggling to stay on her feet, but the dizziness overcame her as pain shot through her skull, and she collapsed into the darkness.

SHE DRAGGED MACY across the floor, cursing herself for letting things get this far.

She should have killed her and burned down this damn house a long time ago. Her secrets were meant to stay hidden, just like that body in the wall, but now Macy was messing it all up.

Her lungs strained for air with the weight of Macy's limp body as she pulled and yanked her to the closet. She opened the door and pushed Macy inside. Huffing to catch her breath, she slammed the door shut, then ran out back where she'd left the gas can earlier.

The thunder still rumbled, but the clouds seemed

to be moving on. Wiping sweat from her forehead with one hand, she carried the gas can inside and poured it around the living room and kitchen.

Stepping back, she set the can beside the closet door, then removed the book of matches from her pocket. The first one struck quickly, and she tossed it toward the old sofa, then struck a few more and threw them onto the gas.

Flames burst to life, then began to catch and creep across the wood floor, eating the rotting wood like kindling.

# *Chapter Fifteen*

Stone was almost home when the 911 call came from the couple who'd bought Kate's former house. A fire had broken out at the Stark place.

He flipped on his siren, then sped toward the house, punching Macy's number as he maneuvered around a pickup and slower traffic. He honked at a car that started through the intersection, then whipped his car to the right to avoid hitting it.

Macy's phone rang four times, then went to voice mail. Dammit, where was she?

Fear clawed at him. Hopefully not at the house…

He hung up and tried her number again but got her voice mail. He glanced at the diner as he passed, looking for her car, scanning the streets and other businesses, but didn't see it anywhere. On the chance she just wasn't answering her phone or the battery was dead, he called the inn.

Celeste answered. "It's the sheriff. Is Macy Stark there?"

"I haven't seen her come in tonight," Celeste said.

Disappointment made him curse. "If she does, have her call me."

Celeste agreed, and he hung up and rounded the turn to the Stark house and barreled up the driveway. Flames were shooting into the dark sky, smoke curling in a gray cloud out a broken window. His pulse jumped when he spotted Macy's car in the drive.

Panicked, he jumped out, shouting Macy's name as he ran toward the house. He couldn't wait for the fire department. Macy might be inside.

"Macy!" Hoping she'd escaped, he glanced all around the outside but didn't see her anywhere. Shouting her name again, he jogged up the steps. The door felt warm but not hot and was ajar.

He looked through the front window and saw flames rippling along the far wall of the living room and in the kitchen. Patches danced around the vinyl sofa and chewed at its legs, climbing upward.

He didn't see Macy in the front. The hall didn't appear to be in flames yet. He eased the door open, the heat and scent of gasoline assaulting him as he stepped inside. "Macy!"

Quickly he scanned the room, then the kitchen. No Macy. Smoke blurred his vision as he darted down the hall, and he coughed, covering his mouth with his hand to keep from inhaling it. He jumped over patches of flames and dashed into the bedrooms but didn't see Macy anywhere.

Fear pulsed through him. Where the hell was she?

Panicked, he checked the closet and bathroom. Empty. The fire was crawling closer, though, the heat growing more intense.

"Macy, where are you?"

Maybe she'd escaped out back.

Judging from the gasoline can, the fire had been set intentionally. She could have caught the person during the act and given chase outside into the woods.

He had to make sure the house was clear, though, so he darted through more shooting flames to go to the basement. But the closet door caught his eye. He pulled at it, but the door seemed stuck. He banged on it and called Macy's name again, beating at the fire eating the floor and door.

He slammed his shoulder into it, then yanked it again and the door finally swung open. His heart stuttered when he spotted Macy slumped on the floor unconscious.

Cold fear knotted his stomach, and he stooped down and scooped her into his arms. He pressed her face into his chest to keep her from being scalded or from inhaling more smoke, then raced through the burning room, dodging plaster crumbling down from the ceiling.

A siren wailed outside, the fire engine roaring into the drive as he ran with her, carrying her away from the inferno. She hung limp, her hair draping his arm as he knelt beneath a tree and gently laid her on the ground.

His heart raced as he felt for a pulse.

MACY'S HEAD THROBBED as if someone was pounding her skull with a hammer. She felt movement and nausea roll through her, then heard a gruff voice calling her name.

"Macy, honey, wake up."

A soft stroke of her hair, and she tried to open her eyes. Loud voices echoed around her. A siren. The wind. Wood popping and crackling.

"Macy, it's Stone. The medics are going to take you to the hospital."

The world blurred, smoke stinging her eyes as she felt herself being lifted. A blanket over her. Gentle hands turning her head, parting her hair, talking over her.

Stone squeezed her hand. "What happened, Macy?"

Confusion clouded her brain, but snippets of her memory returned. "Someone…at the house…hit me."

"Did you see who it was?"

She shook her head, or at least she thought she did. The movement sent another wave of nausea over her, and she swallowed back bile.

"Male? Female?"

"Just a shadow," she whispered.

"Okay, take it easy." He noticed bruises on her hands and arms and wondered if she'd fought her attacker. "I'm going to call a crime team, then I'll meet you at the hospital."

Macy felt his hand squeeze hers, then she was jostled around as the medics loaded her into the ambulance. The siren fired up, screeching and jabbing at the pain in her head like dozens of needles.

She closed her eyes to drown it out and let the darkness pull her under again.

STONE PULLED THE hood of his rain jacket over his head as he watched the firefighters work to extinguish the blaze. He was grateful for their quick action. The clouds had finally unleashed a deluge of rain, which helped to douse the flames, and everyone was soaked.

"We managed to contain the damage to the living room and kitchen," his friend and the chief arson investigator Riggs Benford told him. "Although the smoke and water damage will be significant to the other rooms. What happened?"

His jaw tightened. "Someone knocked Macy unconscious, then put her in the closet and poured gasoline around the room."

Riggs eyes darkened. "They tried to kill her?"

Stone nodded. "Someone doesn't want her investigating the murder that happened here. She received a threat earlier."

"Damn," Riggs said. "Is she okay?"

"She took a hit to the back of her head and probably has a concussion," he said, worry gnawing at him. "But I didn't see any burns. I'm headed to the hospital when I leave here."

The Evidence Response Team arrived, three investigators exiting their van with their kits.

"Fire will have to cool down before we can do much," Riggs told him. "But I'll hang around and oversee the team."

"Thanks. I saw a gas can in there. Maybe you can get some prints."

The ERT approached and Stone explained what had happened. He glanced at the graveled drive and saw tire prints from Macy's car. But no other. "That car belongs to Special Agent Macy Stark," he said. "She was trapped in the closet in the fire and is on her way to the hospital. Look around out here for signs of another vehicle." He pointed to the woods behind the house. "It's possible whoever attacked her left on foot through the woods and had a car parked on the street on the other side."

"We'll be thorough," the lead ERT officer said.

"I'm going to question the neighbor and see if anyone saw a car or person here."

The team began to disperse while the firefighters began stowing their equipment. Smoke still drifted from the debris, the odor of charred wood mingling with the scent of rain.

Stone wiped water from his face, told Riggs to keep him posted, asked him to have one of the officers drop Macy's car at the inn, then he climbed in his squad car. He drove the short distance to the neighbor's house, the one that had once belonged to Kate and her mother. After Kate graduated from college, she'd decided to sell and had bought a new build to start over.

The rain was slacking off as he parked at the ranch house, noting the new owners had done some updates by painting the brick white, adding black trim, and planting colorful flower beds. Kate must be pleased that they were taking such good care of her mother's home.

He walked up to the front door and knocked, Macy's pale face as he'd carried her from the burning house haunting him. A few minutes later, and he would have been too late.

Footsteps sounded inside and the door opened, revealing a young woman holding a toddler on her hip. The little redheaded girl was licking a red Popsicle, the juice dripping down her chin. He'd seen the family around town and knew they had two other children. The father worked at the bank.

"Sheriff?"

"Hi, Mary Sue," Stone said. "I guess you saw the smoke at the house next door."

"I did and called 911," she said. "What happened?"

Stone explained that Macy was there.

"Oh my goodness, is she okay?"

"She's at the hospital," he said, the urge to be with her growing stronger. But Macy would want him to ask questions, find out who'd tried to kill her. "Did you see another vehicle over there tonight? Or a person on foot maybe?"

Mary Sue shook her head. "I'm afraid not. Little Amelia has been sick, so I've been inside with her all day and evening. And Johnny isn't home yet."

Stone gave a quick nod. "How about any time over the last few weeks?"

The toddler rubbed at her eyes as she finished the treat, and Mary Sue took the sticky Popsicle stick. "Sorry, but I haven't. I was shocked to hear about that body being found."

"When Lynn Stark was still living here, did you ever see anything suspicious going on there?"

The woman wrinkled her brow. "I hate to talk ill

of her, but I thought she was troubled, so we kept our distance." Her voice cracked. "I guess I wasn't a very good neighbor."

"You were just taking care of your family," Stone said.

She bit down on her lower lip, then released a breath. "Actually I might have seen something. I should have called it in, but I felt bad for not trying to help that woman out. But now…"

"What are you talking about?" Stone asked.

"I think I saw Lynn at the house earlier today."

Stone's gut clenched. If Macy's mother had been there, could she have set the fire? Would she try to kill her own daughter to keep her secrets?

"Thank you." He hesitated. "If you think of anything else, please give me a call."

She murmured she would, and he rushed back to his car. Fear for Macy made him speed toward the hospital.

If whoever wanted her dead realized Macy had survived the fire, she was still in danger.

MACY ENDURED THE CAT scan and stitches, managing not to pass out again, but her head throbbed, her eyes were burning, and her throat felt raw.

Finally she was settled into a room for the night. As much as she hated hospitals and had asked to go home, the doctor insisted she stay overnight for observation.

The steady sound of machines beeping and medicine and food carts clanging down the hall blended with the staff's voices, and she felt her eyes closing again, the bliss of sleep pulling at her.

In her mind though, flashed an image of the house she'd grown up in and those last few minutes before she'd lost consciousness. The sound of a footstep, the shadow moving across the doorway… had it been a man or a woman?

She clenched the edge of the sheet in frustration, willing some detail to come forward. An image that would give her the answer.

The scent of alcohol and antiseptic from the hospital wafted to her, then the smell of lavender. No… not here. Back at the house when she started inside…

Lavender…her mother used a lavender scented lotion. Once when she was small, she'd gotten into the bottle and slathered her arms and legs with it. For her birthday, when she was four, her mother had given her a bottle all her own.

She clung to that sweet memory as she drifted to sleep, yet the nightmares returned. In that rainstorm…the man in her hallway…her mother screaming, the man's voice…

The next day, her mother staring blankly into space…wailing…yelling at her to go away…

A noise startled her awake, then a soft, husky voice. She opened her eyes, squinting in the dim light, looking up to see Stone's handsome, worried face, his dark eyes studying her. He reached out and brushed her cheek with the back of his hand.

"How do you feel?"

His tenderness brought tears to her eyes. How

long had it been since anyone had really cared about her? Her ex certainly hadn't.

"Macy?"

She swallowed to wet her dry throat. "A headache, sore throat. I'll be okay."

A small smile of understanding passed across his broad chiseled face. "What did the doctor say?"

"A slight concussion. I wanted to go to the inn, but he insisted I stay for observation." She tried to sit up and winced, a coughing spell overcoming her.

Stone handed her the cup of water on the bedside table, and she took a long, slow drink. The water felt good on her throat as it went down.

Stone took the cup when she was finished and she sank back, exhausted. "Did you find anything at the house?"

"Forensics are processing the scene now, and Riggs is overseeing the arson investigation. There was a gas can left there. Maybe it'll yield something." He ran a hand through his hair. "Do you remember anything?"

"I took some of my mother's papers out to the car to look through later. When I turned, I saw a shadowy figure in the house and went to check it out." She paused, struggling again for details. "I couldn't tell if it was a man or a woman. But… I think I smelled lavender."

"Lavender?"

Macy nodded. "My mother used to have lavender lotion. The strange thing is that I hadn't smelled it before in the house since I got back."

His eyes narrowed, worry flickering in the dark depths.

Macy's pulse jumped. "What is it? Do you know something you're not telling me?"

Stone looked away. "We can talk about it tomorrow after you're feeling better."

Macy reached for his hand. "Tell me, Stone. Don't hold back."

He cleared his throat, his eyes filled with concern. "The lady who bought Kate's house said she saw your mother at your place earlier today."

Macy's chest clenched. Had her mother set the fire and tried to kill her?

# *Chapter Sixteen*

Stone hated the pain in Macy's eyes. He should have kept his mouth shut tonight. Given her time to recover before he dropped that bombshell.

The very idea that her own mother would try to kill her had to come as a shock. Or had she already considered the possibility? What else wasn't she telling him about Lynn Stark?

"Do you want to talk about it?" he asked.

She shook her head. "What is there to discuss? I know my mother has personality disorders and can be violent. If she's scared now of getting caught for something she did years ago, it could push her over the edge."

"But to lash out at you?" he said, unable to keep the disbelief from his voice. "She's your mother, for God's sake. There has to be another explanation."

Macy rubbed her temple, her eyes drooping, and he tamped down his outrage. "I'm sorry, Macy."

She looked up at him with such emotion that his heart squeezed, and he gently stroked her cheek. More than anything he wanted to make things right for her. But he had no idea how to do that.

*Maybe you can find Lynn and prove she didn't try to burn down the house with Macy inside.*

But what if she had? How in the world would Macy live with that?

"You need to rest now," he said softly. "We can talk tomorrow when you're feeling better."

"I am tired," she admitted. "You can go."

He stroked her cheek again, and her eyes fluttered, then closed. He didn't intend to leave her alone, not knowing someone had tried to kill her. If the culprit realized she'd survived, he or she might come back to finish the job. "Just rest, Macy," he murmured.

Although he didn't think she heard him. She'd already drifted to sleep.

He stared at her for a long minute, his heart hammering with admiration and worry. Macy acted tough, but she had a vulnerable side. She just covered it up because she'd had to in order to survive.

In his mind, he saw her as a teenager. Quiet. Studious. An athlete. He'd watched her run track and remembered she was fast, that she blew by some of the other girls. The hundred-meter was her best event, and she always brought up the rear in the relays. She'd taken the school to the state championships. She'd been humble when praised, but she'd had a dogged competitive spirit and intense concentration.

Maybe because she was blocking out her terrible home life.

At least on the track she'd found accolades. Although he never saw her hanging out with the other girls afterward.

His phone buzzed. A text from Forensics: Prints on the gun case and rock used to break the window at the pawnshop belong to Lynn Stark.

He ran a hand over his face, his stomach churning. So not only had she been seen at the Stark house today, before the attack on Macy, but she'd stolen firearms after she'd escaped the psychiatric center.

Which meant she was armed and dangerous.

THE NIGHTMARES AND memories assaulted Macy in confusing snippets as she slept. She saw her mother slipping into the shadows of the house earlier. Heard her whispered warnings not to go in the basement. Saw her passed out on the kitchen floor half-naked with a bottle of pills beside her.

But even in her dreams with the haunting realization that her mother had actually been at the house, she fought the ugly possibility that her mother had dragged her in that closet and planned to burn her alive.

She moaned and rolled to her side, nausea building. Her eyes opened and then closed, the pain in her head so intense she begged for sleep to sweep her away again.

Another memory floated through her subconscious, launching her back in time. *She was seven years old, and she woke up to the sound of her mother's voice. When she tiptoed to the kitchen, her mother was dancing around and singing into the rolling pin as if it were a microphone. When she saw Macy, she laughed, took her hands, and they danced around together in their pajamas. Then they ate pizza and had Coke floats for breakfast on a picnic cloth in front of the TV and watched cartoons.*

*"We're going to the carnival now," her mother said. "And then we'll get ice cream and go shopping and buy you the prettiest dress you've ever seen."*

*Macy didn't want dresses, but her mother was so happy and excited that she didn't dare say so.*

*They got dressed quickly, then drove to the carnival, and her mother squealed and laughed like a child as they rode ride after ride, and then her mother won a giant panda bear for her in a ring-toss game. They gorged on ice cream and cotton candy.*

*But when they went to town and walked toward the dress store, they passed a coffee shop and her mother suddenly halted. For a long minute, she stared through the window at a couple inside laughing and holding hands.*

*Then suddenly a dark shadow fell over her. She stiffened, snatched Macy's hand and dragged her away. She squeezed Macy's hand so tightly Macy cried out. But that only made her mother madder, and she yelled at Macy to shut up.*

*"Don't be a baby," her mother snapped as she yanked her to the car.*

*Macy's lip quivered as tears trickled down her face, and she couldn't help but cry.*

*"I said shut up!" her mother screamed. "Shut up!"*

*Macy buried her head into her hands and pressed her fist to her mouth to keep from sobbing out loud as her mother drove like a maniac home. When they got there, her mother threw the panda bear in the trash outside, and shoved Macy into her room and locked the door.*

Macy jerked her eyes open, disoriented, a sick feeling overwhelming her. A low sound echoed around her, and for a moment, she was so disoriented she struggled to recall where she was.

But slowly reality returned and the ugly truth hit her. She was in the hospital. Someone wanted her dead.

Pulse quickening, she rolled to her back again, then looked up and saw Stone in the recliner beside the bed, his head lolled to the side. The noise she'd heard was his soft snoring.

A five-o'clock shadow grazed his wide jaw, his button-down shirt stretched across his thick muscled chest, accentuating his broad shoulders, and a lock of his brown hair fell across his forehead.

She should wake him and tell him to leave. But the fear pounding her chest was relentless, and he looked so sexy in that chair, that he made her feel safe.

It had been a long time since she'd felt safe.

So she closed her eyes again and allowed sleep to claim her, praying that the nightmares would leave her alone for a little while. But she knew they'd be back.

Still, she'd face them in the morning.

STONE WOKE THE next morning with a crick in his neck, the sound of medicine carts, nurses' voices and hospital machinery echoing from the halls.

He'd kept one eye half-open most of the night in case Macy's attacker showed up, but thankfully no one except the staff had come into the room. And they had been in plenty of times to take Macy's vitals. How anyone rested in a hospital was beyond him.

He rolled his shoulders and neck to work out the knots. But one look at Macy's pale face as she tossed and turned in the hospital bed and he knew staying with her had been worth it.

At least she was safe.

Although she appeared to be in the throes of a nightmare.

"No..." she cried. "Please stop..."

The pain in her cry tore at him, and he rubbed his hand over his bleary eyes, then gently stroked the hair from her forehead. "Macy, wake up, honey," he murmured. "You're having a bad dream."

She clenched the sheet in a white-knuckle grip, drawing his attention to the bruises on her hands and arms again as she slowly opened her eyes. He hoped to hell the forensics team found the attacker's DNA beneath her nails. Then he could track down the animal who'd hurt Macy and lock him or her up.

"You stayed all night?" Macy said in a raw whisper.

She sounded surprised.

"Of course," he said. "I'm not leaving you alone again until we find the person who set that fire."

Emotions glittered in her eyes, but the doctor came in before she could speak.

"How are you feeling this morning?" the doctor asked as she reviewed Macy's chart.

Macy lifted her chin. “Fine. I’m ready to be discharged.”

The doctor quirked a brow, a glint in her eye. “I’m sure you are. But you did sustain a contusion on the back of your head.” She tapped the chart. “Your vitals look good, but you need to rest another day. If I release you, I don’t know that will happen.”

Macy opened her mouth to argue, but Stone cut her off. “She will. I will watch over her myself.”

Macy shot him a venomous look, but he simply graced her with a challenging smile as if to say it was the hospital or him. Her choice. The only way to deal with her, he realized. She did not like to be out of control.

He could relate to that.

“Macy? You are coming home with me—” he paused for emphasis “—under protective custody, of course.”

That earned him another glare, but she released a resigned sigh. “All right. I just want to get out of here. Who the hell can sleep with people coming in all hours of the night waking you up to make sure you’re breathing?”

Her exasperation made his lips twitch with a tiny smile, but he didn’t dare comment. He liked the fire in Macy, liked her athleticism and grit.

“Fine,” the doctor said. “I’ll sign release papers. But if you experience dizziness, nausea or disorientation, give me a call.”

“I know the drill,” Macy said drily. “It’s not the first concussion I’ve had.”

New concern flickered in the doctor's eyes. "Then maybe we should run more tests."

Macy was already pushing the sheets away. "I only meant that I understand the symptoms. And of course I'll call you if I have problems." She gave the doctor a saccharine smile that neither the doctor nor Stone was buying.

All the more reason he would not let her out of his sight for the next few days. He didn't intend to let anything happen to Macy on his watch.

MACY KNEW SHE was being stubborn, but she hadn't survived her life by being a wimp, and she didn't intend to start now. She wanted answers, and she was damn well going to get them. Even if it meant putting up with Stone's protective attitude a little while longer.

Her ex had never been protective. Trey was a taker, not a giver. She'd been a fool to believe anything else.

Stone excused himself to make a call while she signed dismissal papers. The medics or nurses, she couldn't remember which, had stripped her clothes and she knew Stone would have sent them to Forensics, which she would have done herself. So she was wearing scrubs back to the inn.

Maybe she could convince Stone to leave her there.

He looked somber when he returned and lapsed into a brooding mood as he drove her back to the inn.

"Stone, I'll really be fine here at Celeste's," she said as he escorted her to her room.

"You're staying with me until we catch whoever attacked you," he said. "You know two heads are better than one. I may be more objective than you."

She tensed, an argument building in her mind.

"And before you say I'm being controlling," Stone said, "remember that we worked well together to uncover the person threatening Kate and what really happened with Ned Hodgkins. I also vowed to protect the citizens of Briar Ridge, and that means anyone visiting or passing through, too."

Damn, he made a compelling case. She blinked, biting her tongue. But she didn't like exposing herself and her family secrets.

What other choice did she have, though? He *had* saved her life. And although her mother had hurt her, her emotions were all over the place. She might have a blind spot when it came to her.

She could not afford that.

Her job was all she had left.

"All right. But let me get those papers out of my car," she said, grateful she'd confiscated them before the fire.

The hair on the back of her neck prickled. Then again, if the papers held a clue, it was possible that whoever set that fire could have wanted to dispose of them.

Hope battled through the hazy fog of despair eating at her. She'd look at them as soon as they reached Stone's house.

# *Chapter Seventeen*

"Pack everything you'll need for a few days," Stone said as he stood at the door to Macy's room. "You can stay at my place as long as you want. And in case you're worried, I have two bedrooms, so you'll have your own room and bath."

Macy's heart fluttered. She'd wondered about that. She entered the room, still hesitant. "Stone, I would be safe here."

"Don't argue with me," Stone said. "I can't work if I don't know you're safe. And…there's something else I have to tell you."

Her heart skipped a beat at the intensity in his eyes. "What is it?"

"Prints from the pawnshop where the guns were stolen match your mother's."

Macy's breath caught. "Then she's armed."

He nodded. "Armed and maybe panicked. You know what a dangerous combination that is."

Macy stewed over that information. "If she had a gun, why set fire to the house? Why not shoot me?"

"To get rid of forensics," he said matter-of-factly.

A shudder rippled through her. She didn't want

to believe that her mother would kill her, but she couldn't ignore facts.

Resigned, she went to the bathroom and packed her toiletries, then gathered her suitcase. Stone insisted on carrying it outside.

"I'll take my car," Macy said as she reached for her keys.

"You're not driving today, not after the head injury," Stone said bluntly. "Besides, leaving your car here could throw off whoever is looking for you. If they see it at my place, they'll know where you are."

He had a point.

"Okay, let me get those papers and the notes I've made on the case so far."

He stowed her luggage in the trunk of his police car while she grabbed her computer bag, her notes on the investigation and the box of paperwork she'd taken from her mother's house.

Her head was throbbing as he drove away from the inn, and she stayed in the car as he stopped at the diner to pick them up breakfast and coffee. The sidewalks were already filling with locals and tourists for the upcoming Fourth festivities, and children laughed and chased each other in the park in the center of town.

Across the street, she spotted a woman with curly brown hair pushing a swing with a young girl in it, and it took her back to her childhood. Except she didn't remember her mother ever bringing her here. Kate's mother had.

Another woman caught her eye as she slipped

into the shadows, and her pulse quickened. Was that her mother ducking into a side street?

She reached for the door handle to climb out and give chase, then the woman turned, and Macy blinked her into focus. Not her mother.

Good grief. She was being paranoid.

Stone returned a moment later with bags of food and hot coffee, and she inhaled the rich scents, then added sweetener to her coffee. One swig and her throbbing head already felt better.

Five minutes later, Stone pulled down a long drive to a log cabin on the creek that looked rustic and charming with the pines, live oaks and mountains in the background. Crepe myrtles and hydrangeas added color to the landscaping, and the front porch held rocking chairs.

"This is beautiful," Macy said.

Stone's look turned sheepish. "Thanks. I had it built a few years ago. Needed to be close to town but not in the house where I grew up."

Macy nodded in understanding.

They got out in silence, and she carried the food and her computer bag while he snagged her luggage. When Macy entered, she was struck by the ten-foot ceilings, floor to ceiling windows across the back of the living room that offered a view of the steep ridges and overhangs of the mountains. His furnishings were simple: leather sofa, comfy club chairs, a blanket tossed across the back of the couch. The space was open concept with granite counters, rich wood cabinets, a large breakfast island and rustic beams.

"Wow," she said, impressed. "This is really nice." And very private, she thought. Much like Stone himself.

Stone shrugged. "I like it." He gestured toward the right. "Guest room is on that side. Mine is on the other."

Macy followed him to a bedroom that held a black iron bed covered in a log cabin quilt with an adjoining bathroom. A claw-foot tub was the centerpiece. Both spaces looked as if they hadn't been used, suggesting he rarely had guests.

He placed her suitcase on a luggage rack in the corner of the bedroom, then paused at the doorway and gestured toward his clothes. "I reek of smoke, and I'm sure you'd like a hot shower."

She looked down at the scrubs, still feeling dirty from the attack the night before. Her hair smelled like smoke and was matted from where she'd bled. "That would be great. Then we can eat and look through those papers."

"Sounds like a plan."

He stepped from the room, and Macy rolled her shoulders, then closed the door. She pulled fresh clothes from her bag, settled her toiletries in the bathroom, then looked at the tub that beckoned. A long hot bath would soothe her aches and pains.But she didn't have time to indulge herself. For now she turned on the shower water, stripped and climbed inside. But as the water sluiced over her, she closed her eyes and tried to recall more details about the attack.

The scent of the lavender…the neighbor had seen her mother at the house. Her mother with a gun…

A dead hit man in the basement. The fact that her mother had taken lovers—or a lover—who she knew nothing about.

Suddenly antsy to get back to work, she dried off, combed through her damp hair, and dressed in a pair of jeans and a T-shirt. Then she hurried into the kitchen for more coffee, food, and to look at those papers her mother had held on to.

But when she entered the living room, Kate and Brynn were there. Stone gave her an apologetic look. "They heard about the incident at your house." He gestured to the coffeepot. "Help yourself. I'll be back." He disappeared into his bedroom, and Kate rushed to Macy and pulled her toward the sofa. A peacefulness fell over Macy like a warm blanket. Macy had loved Kate the minute she'd let her sleep in her room that first night she'd found her outside her house in the storm. Although Kate had always been self-conscious of her curves, Macy thought they were gorgeous, and her auburn hair was as glassy as a pony's. Plus she was loving, kind and compassionate, just like her mother had been.

Brynn had already parked her wheelchair beside the couch and held a mug of coffee. Even though she looked worried, her blond hair made her look like an angel. In spite of her mother's ill attitude, Brynn had always been pretty on the inside as she was on the outside. "We've been worried sick about you," Brynn said, her voice cracking.

Kate squeezed her hands, and Macy fought tears.

"Are you okay, Macy?' Brynn asked. "Riggs told me what happened last night."

Macy breathed out, glad she'd at least showered the stench of smoke and blood off her. "I'm fine. But it was a long night."

Kate went and poured the two of them coffee, and Macy cradled the cup between her hands.

"What happened?" Brynn asked.

Macy inhaled a fortifying breath and explained the information she'd gleaned so far.

Kate's expression faltered, and Brynn glanced at Stone's closed door. "Is there something going on between you and Stone?"

Macy's heart fluttered. For a brief second as she glanced around the cozy home and thought of Stone staying with her all night, she longed for more. But she gave a small shake of her head. "He's just doing his job, assigned himself as my bodyguard."

A heartbeat passed, and Kate leaned forward. "I know your mother had issues, Macy. But I can't believe she'd actually try to kill you. Have you considered that Trey might have tried to hurt you?"

Macy jerked her head up. "I guess it's possible. He was furious over the divorce and the arrest."

"Has he threatened you?" Brynn asked.

Macy hesitated. "He's left angry messages, but I assumed it was all smoke." Maybe she should have taken the threats more seriously.

"Did you tell Stone?" Kate asked.

Macy shook her head. "I've been so caught up in finding my mother and what happened with that body that I just blew it off."

But the wheels in her head started spinning. If Trey had seen the news about the murder at her house, he could have come after her for revenge, knowing she'd be looking at the dead body and her mother for answers, and not at him as a threat.

STONE HADN'T MEANT to eavesdrop, but he heard Kate ask Macy if anything was going on with the two of them, and she'd denied it.

He wasn't so sure about that. Although maybe the attraction was all one-sided.

But the question about her ex disturbed him. He'd been so caught up in the murder at the Stark house and Macy's mother's disappearance that it hadn't occurred to him that Trey might have retaliated against Macy.

And why hadn't she told him about the threats?

He showered quickly, then dressed in clean jeans and a button-down white shirt and decided to find Trey. He made a quick call to his deputy. "Bridges, see if you can locate Trey Cushing. I want him brought in for questioning."

"Cushing? Isn't he that special agent's ex-husband?" Murphy asked.

"He is," Stone replied. "She arrested him a few weeks ago, but he was released. Apparently he's been leaving her threatening messages."

"You think he may have attacked her at that house and set the fire?"

"I don't know," Stone said. "He has a temper and told her she'd be sorry for humiliating him. Call the lab and asked him to compare his DNA with forensics they found at the Stark house."

"Copy that. Any ideas where Cushing is?" Bridges asked.

"No, but call local motels. He didn't have any family left in town, and he sure as hell didn't have friends. Also check DMV records for an address in case he has property somewhere in the area." He drummed his fingers on his thigh. "He drives a black Ford truck. I'm not sure about the license plate, but see if you can find it."

"On it," Bridges agreed. "By the way, Gretta has already called, demanding an interview about the fire and the murder case."

"Stall her," Stone said. "Macy needs time to recover, and I need time to investigate without Gretta breathing down my neck. She'll just create panic in town."

Bridges agreed, and Stone ended the call, then went to join Macy and her friends.

"When this is over and you're safe, we need to look for bridesmaids dresses," Kate said. "I was thinking that you and Brynn can wear a little black dress, any style you like."

Macy gave Kate a smile, although she was tracing her finger along the rim of her coffee mug as if distracted.

"I'm sorry," Kate said. "I guess it seems insensitive for me to talk about wedding plans when you're going through so much."

Macy shook her head. "No, we spent too much

time apart. I'm happy for you, Kate. Planning your wedding is something to look forward to."

Stone wondered about her own wedding to Cushing. What had gone wrong? Would she ever consider marriage again?

He shook away the thoughts. Now was not the time to consider a personal relationship. He had to protect her and help her put her life back together.

Then she'd leave. But at least when she did, he'd know she was safe. That would have to be enough.

AS SOON AS Kate and Brynn left, Stone heated their sausage and biscuits, and they devoured them. Macy was surprised that she was hungry, then realized she hadn't eaten the night before.

"Why didn't you tell me about Cushing's threats?" he asked.

Macy paused, her coffee cup halfway to her mouth. "I guess I didn't think he'd follow through," she said. "You know Trey is a lot of talk and posturing."

"But threats?" Stone's dark gaze met hers. "Considering the circumstances, Macy, we have to consider that he meant them. Getting arrested in front of our class could have put him over the edge."

Pain clenched her chest. "I know that."

"Do you think he's capable of violence?"

Doubts assailed her along with memories of his outbursts when he didn't get his way. "He does have a temper. Maybe we should talk to him."

"I've already asked my deputy to find him and bring him in for questioning," Stone said. "And

Macy, we're working together. You have to trust me. Don't keep anything else from me."

Macy gave a little nod, although it was still difficult for her to talk about Trey. She'd been so foolish…

Turning back to the case, she opened the box of her mother's papers and organized them into piles. "There are bills, bank statements and checkbooks going all the way back thirty years," she said. Her mother had been a pack rat.

"Your mother kept all this?" Stone said.

Macy made a low sound in her throat. "She wasn't exactly organized," she said, thinking about her chaotic ways. "At least here's the deed to the house," she said, then studied it. "It was paid off."

Stone arched a brow. "That surprises me. How did she do that on a housekeeper's salary?"

Macy shook her head, curious herself. "Good question. I know she worked when I was little, but in high school, I don't remember her being employed on a regular basis. By then, she was too… unstable."

"I'll look through her bills if you want to start searching her financials," Stone offered.

Macy nodded and began sorting and stacking the bank statements in order of month and year to make comparisons. She used a legal pad to list names of accounts and amounts paid to her mother in one column, then in another column listed payments her mother had made.

On another sheet she wrote the names of everyone she knew of that her mother had cleaned for and the years she'd worked for the clients so she could match those names to the ones in the bank statements.

It was a painstakingly slow process as she combed through statement after statement. While some of her clients had paid with a check, there were cash deposits that she couldn't trace.

The list of clients:

Beverly Jones
Ken and Pat Dansing
Vicki Germaine
Troy and Shirley Cregan
Dodie Lewis
Loretta Pruitt
Prentice and Adeline Walkman

She searched for discrepancies and found payments from Beverly, the Dansings, the Cregans, Loretta Pruitt and the Walkmans. There was nothing from Dodie Lewis, suggesting she probably paid in cash. The payments were what she would have expected for a maid, although it appeared the Walkmans had paid almost double the others.

It could have been due to the fact that their house was larger, she supposed. Or perhaps she did more in-depth cleaning for the couple. They also seemed more consistent, and she'd been paid weekly whereas the others ranged between twice a month and once a month.

The time frames and payments coincided with

what her clients had told Macy. She'd begun working for the Walkmans the year before Macy was born.

Their son had died earlier that same year.

Her skin prickled with unease. Something about the dates seemed curious. But it made sense that if they'd lost a child, they would have been distraught and needed help around the house.

Her eyes grew blurry from studying the numbers and she stood and stretched, then went and got more coffee. "Do you want another cup?" she asked Stone, who was still scouring the stacks and stacks of bills.

"Yeah, thanks," he said.

Macy poured them both a mug and carried it to him. The gesture and close quarters felt somehow intimate, although Stone seemed oblivious. Instead, his brow furrowed as he opened another envelope, removed the contents and studied them.

Macy looked over his shoulder. "What is that?"

"Paperwork noting that your mother's house was paid off." He pointed to the date. "It looks like a lump sum of seventy thousand dollars was sent to the mortgage company."

Macy leaned closer and noted the date, and her heart hammered. "It was paid off on my first birthday." She glanced at Stone. "The question is—where did she get that kind of money?"

# *Chapter Eighteen*

Stone didn't know Macy's mother well enough to be able to answer that. But the large cash deposit was definitely suspicious. "Did your mother have any family? Perhaps a relative who passed who might have left her the money?"

Macy rubbed her forehead in thought. "Not that I know of. She said her parents died when she was sixteen and she became a ward of the state. And I don't remember her ever talking about other relatives."

"Maybe she did but they were estranged," Stone suggested.

"With her condition, that would make sense," Macy agreed.

"Let me keep looking through her papers," he said. "I'll also search county records to see if she received any kind of inheritance."

"An inheritance wouldn't have been paid out in cash, though," Macy pointed out.

Stone stewed over that. "True. Unless it was paid to a second party, say a relative or sibling who divided it up and gave your mother her share in cash."

"Look into it," Macy said, although she didn't seem convinced. "There's another answer, you know."

Stone's gaze met hers, turmoil darkening her eyes. "Your father?"

"It would fit. He didn't want anything to do with me, so he paid her to keep quiet."

"Yet he provided the two of you with a home," Stone said in an attempt to soften the blow.

Macy shrugged. She couldn't really call that house a home. "I'll keep looking through the bank statements and her calendar to see if she might have visited the prison to see Hubert."

They settled back in for another hour, then Stone stepped onto the back deck and phoned County Records. He asked to speak to Tammy, whom he'd known for years, and explained that he needed information on Lynn Stark, specifically if there were records of her receiving any kind of inheritance.

"I'll see what I can find out and get back to you," Tammy said.

He thanked her, then returned to his computer and ran a background search on Lynn Stark, looking for her birth certificate. She was born in Asheville to Tim and Betty Stark on November 1. Father worked at the carpet mills and mother worked as a cashier at a quick mart.

Just as she'd told Macy, her parents died when she was sixteen and she'd become a ward of the state. At eighteen she'd left the group home and… there wasn't much of a paper trail after that. She had worked at a grocery store for a while, then moved to Briar Ridge, where she'd given birth to Macy at Briar Ridge Hospital.

"When do the checks for housekeeping services start?" he asked Macy.

She checked her list. "The year before I was born." Macy thumped her finger on one of the statements. "You know this is strange."

"What?" Stone asked.

She glanced at her notes, making comparisons between the spreadsheets she was creating. "There are two payments from the Walkmans that were entered after they said they moved away."

Stone frowned. He didn't know what that meant, but it was worth asking about.

His phone buzzed. His deputy. "I need to answer this."

He left her studying the statements while he answered the call. "Sheriff."

"I found Cushing," Murphy said. "I'm bringing him in."

Stone's stomach clenched. "I'll be right there."

THE NUMBERS AND timing of payments were still bugging Macy, but her head was throbbing again so she downed two painkillers and chugged a glass of water.

"My deputy brought Cushing in," Stone said as he hung up the phone. "I'm going to talk to him now."

Macy sucked in a breath and stood. "I'll go with you."

Stone's gaze met hers. "Are you sure that's a good idea? I can handle it."

"I've known Trey a lot longer. I can tell when he's lying." And if he wanted to kill her, she wanted to confront him. She deserved that after putting up with his moodiness during that first year of marriage. And then his overbearing attitude when they'd split. He'd thought he could bully her into coming back to him.

But once she'd made up her mind, there was no turning back.

Stone conceded, and she grabbed her purse and weapon and strapped it on, then followed Stone outside to his car. The bright sunlight hurt her eyes, and she closed them as he drove to the police station.

"Are you sure you're okay, Macy?" he asked gruffly. "If you need to go back and lie down and rest, you can."

"I'm fine," she said, although the winding road was making her slightly nauseated.

Five minutes later, he parked at the station.

"Dammit, Gretta is here," Stone muttered.

A frisson of nerves danced up Macy's spine as she spotted the reporter's BMW. "I swear that woman knows when a crime happened before it happens."

Stone chuckled, and they got out and walked up to the entrance. She squared her shoulders as they entered, bracing herself to contain her emotions as the vulture of a woman made a beeline straight toward her. Deputy Bridges stood from behind his desk with a shake of his head as if to say he had no control over Gretta.

"Macy, are you okay? I heard someone tried to

kill you last night. That's horrible," Gretta said, her tone concerned.

Macy recognized her fake smile for what it was. A ploy to finagle information from her.

"I'm fine," Macy said with a curt smile.

Stone interceded. "If you're here for a news report, we can't comment on an ongoing investigation."

Gretta feigned an innocent look. "Well, the public does deserve to know what's going on," she said, her eyes sparking with determination. "If there's a predator in town, they should be warned."

Macy gritted her teeth. She couldn't argue with that, but she knew it was Gretta's way of manipulating them into talking.

"Gretta, we have work to do," Stone said. "We'll let you know when we're ready to give a statement."

She turned to Macy with an eyebrow raise. "Special Agent Stark?"

Macy folded her arms. "As the sheriff said, we will contact you when we have a statement."

She gave Gretta a saccharine smile, then pushed past her. A gleam of approval flickered in Stone's eyes as he gestured to his deputy to get Trey. He led her past his receptionist's desk, then through a set of double doors to an interrogation room.

A minute later, the deputy escorted Trey inside. He was fuming as he strode across the room. "What the hell are you doing?" he shouted at Macy.

"Sit down," Stone said. "We just want to talk."

Trey flung his hands angrily. "Then why drag me here and put me in a holding cell?" Trey bit out. "Humiliating me in front of the town wasn't enough for you, Macy? You want revenge because your bogus charges didn't stick?"

Macy schooled her reaction by squaring her shoulders. "Where were you last night, Trey?"

He narrowed his eyes. "What? What business is it of yours? You divorced me, remember?"

Stone's boots clicked on the floor as he crossed to stand in front of Trey. "I said *sit down*. This won't take long."

Trey glanced back and forth between them, tension radiating from his rigid movements. He sank into the chair with a thud. "What the hell is this about?" Trey barked.

Stone leaned over Trey and pinned him with an intimidating look. "Answer the question. Where were you last night?"

Trey heaved a long, labored breath, his look seething. "I knew you were a cold bitch, Macy. But not cold enough to try to pin attempted murder or arson on me."

Macy crossed her arms. So he did know about the fire and that she'd been assaulted. "*Where* were you?"

He cut his eyes toward Stone, then back at her, his jaw clenched. "As a matter of fact, I was in bed with another woman." His eyes flickered with satisfaction as if he thought she cared.

He was wrong. She pulled a small notepad from her pocket and pushed it toward him. "Write down her name and contact information."

"You jealous, babe?"

Macy gave a wry laugh. "You wish. All I want is the truth, Trey. And to get you out of my life for good."

He angled his head toward her. "And that's all I want from you. To be rid of you for good, too."

The underlying threat in his tone was meant to frighten her. But Macy had long ago stopped being afraid of Trey. Although she would check into his story.

And if he'd taken advantage of the murder investigation to try to kill her, she'd make sure he was locked up tight.

STONE HAD NEVER liked Trey Cushing, but his opinion of the man kept diving lower and lower. He liked to bully those smaller and more vulnerable than him. He always had.

At least Macy had stood up to him.

But at what cost?

Would Cushing actually try to kill her?

Some men were so obsessive about a woman they would do anything to keep her from being with someone else. Was that what had happened here?

Cushing scribbled down the name Desiree Memes and her cell phone number, and Macy reached for it.

"Who is she, Trey? Another hooker?" Macy asked drily.

That told Stone a lot about their marriage. Not only was Trey a bully but a cheater.

"Don't *you* want to know," Trey teased in a singsongy voice.

Macy shook her head in disgust, and Stone motioned for her to follow him. He'd let Cushing stew while he verified his story.

In the hall, Stone took the name from Macy. "I'll follow up on this."

"Stone, I can do it," Macy said.

"Let me do this for you, Macy." He squeezed her arm gently. "Take my office. Keep working on the case."

Macy nodded, relieved she wouldn't have to hear the sordid details of Trey's night with his lover. That is, if he was telling the truth and his alibi checked out. Knowing him, he could have persuaded some woman to cover for him.

She carried her computer bag and the files she'd been looking at into Stone's office and settled behind the small table in the corner. The payments from the Walkmans that had continued after she was dismissed still perplexed her. Although the family could have simply been generous and given her some kind of severance pay.

The lump sum payment also stumped her. None of the people she'd cleaned for would have had that kind of money. Except for the Walkmans.

But why would they pay off her mother's loan? She'd seen them campaigning for senate and they were all over the place raising money for children's charities, a passion they'd obviously developed after they'd lost their son. Had they felt sorry for her mother and adopted her as a charity project back then?

She wished she could take a look at their financial records, but that would require either a warrant, which she had no justification for, or hacking into their accounts.

She couldn't justify a desperate move like that at this time.

Deciding to find out more about the couple, she called Loretta Pruitt, the woman who'd run the day care.

"What can I do for you?" Loretta asked.

"I'm still talking to everyone my mother worked for. I wondered what you could tell me about the Walkmans. Was my mother working for them when they lost their son?"

A heartbeat passed. "No, she started there a few months after. A young girl named Esme cleaned for them before that. But a couple of months after they lost their child, Esme left for some reason. That's when they hired your mama."

"Does Esme still live around here?" Macy asked.

"Last I heard she got married and moved about thirty miles north."

"Do you know her married name?"

Loretta hesitated. "Frances. Man's first name was Buddy." She gave a soft laugh. "I remember thinking Frances was unusual for a last name."

"What did you think of the Walkmans themselves?"

Another heartbeat. "I'm not sure why you're asking all this. But they seemed like a nice couple. Were devoted to that little boy. It nearly destroyed them when they lost him."

Macy thanked her, then ended the call and used her laptop to run a search for Esme and Buddy Frances. She ran a background check but neither had a police record. DMV found them both. They were still married and lived in an area of the mountains called Woody Creek.

A further search and she found they owned a food truck called Nacho Mama's. She punched the number for the truck and a man answered. She could hear pans banging and voices as if they were busy.

"May I speak to Esme?" Macy asked.

"Sure, hang on," the man said.

More voices and clatter in the truck, and several dings signaling an order was up. Finally Esme answered. "This is Esme. You want to place a to-go order?"

"No, thanks," Macy said, then identified herself. "I'm just looking for some information about Adeline and Prentice Walkman."

"Listen, if you're a reporter, I got nothing to say," Esme said, her voice agitated. "I know how this goes. Press trying to dig up dirt on them because he's running for senate."

"I'm with the FBI and am investigating a cold case in Briar Ridge, which involved a woman named Lynn Stark. I understand that years ago she cleaned for Adeline and Prentice Walkman, and that you worked for them before she did."

Esme's breathing rattled over the line. "I don't understand."

"I'm just collecting background information. I know they paid Ms. Stark well and wondered if you had the same experience."

A tense second passed. "They paid me for cleaning. That's all."

Macy went still, her choice of wording striking

her as odd. Was she implying that they paid her mother for something else?

"I was sorry to hear that they lost a child," Macy said, trying another tactic. "I'm sure that was a difficult time."

"It was terrible," Esme said, her voice filled with sympathy. "As expected, they both took the boy's death extremely hard. Lots of guilt and blame going around. Mrs. Walkman became depressed and withdrawn. Her husband tried to reach her, but his wife seemed too deep in grief to accept comfort."

"That is sad, but it's not uncommon for couples who lose a child to drift apart." She waited, hoping Esme would offer more, but she seemed hesitant to speak. "Why did you leave, exactly?"

"I…really can't say," Esme said. "I just needed a change." Someone shouted in the background, and Esme cleared her throat. "Sorry I can't help you. I have to go. We're really busy right now. Got a line a half mile long for lunch."

Macy thanked her, but her mind was churning as she ended the call and replayed the conversation in her head. As an agent, she'd become adept at reading the nuances of people's gestures, inflections in their tones and the things they didn't say.

Esme was holding something back. To protect herself or the Walkmans?

# *Chapter Nineteen*

Stone halfway hoped Trey's alibi did not check out. He wanted to lock the bastard up for threatening Macy and make sure he stayed away from her.

But he was a lawman, and if he crossed the line, he'd lose the respect of the town. And himself. And possibly Macy.

And that was starting to matter to him more than he wanted to admit.

So he left Cushing to sweat it out, stepped into the second interrogation room and called the number Trey had given. The woman's name was Desiree Memes. Seriously.

At least his deputy had taken Cushing off guard so he hadn't had a chance to call and give the woman a heads-up.

Although if Trey had planned his revenge on Macy, he could have orchestrated an alibi in advance.

The phone rang three times before a woman picked up and said hello.

"This is Sheriff Lawson in Briar Ridge," Stone said. "Is this Desiree?"

A nervous cough echoed back. “Yes. Am I in trouble, Sherriff?”

“I don’t know. Are you?”

“No, I mean I haven’t done anything wrong.”

Still, anxiety laced her voice. “I need you to tell me where you were yesterday from 5:00 p.m. on.”

An awkward pause. “What is this about?”

“Just routine questions,” he said bluntly. “You can answer now, or I can pick you up and bring you in to the station and we can talk here.”

A voice echoed in the background, someone calling her name.

“Listen, my husband is home. He can’t hear this.”

Stone shook his head in disgust. “Then tell me the truth.”

Her sharp intake of breath echoed back, a breath filled with apprehension. “I was with Trey Cushing,” she said. “We…met after the reunion in town a few weeks ago and have been seeing each other since.” Her voice cracked. “But please, you can’t tell my husband. There’s no telling what he’d do.”

Dammit. She truly sounded scared. But she’d just admitted to having an affair and given Trey Cushing an alibi at the same time.

“You were with him all evening and night?” Stone asked.

Another awkward second passed. “Yes, he got a room at the motel outside of town. My husband was on a long haul and just got back.”

Did no one treat their marriage vows as sacred anymore?

“If I learn you’re lying,” Stone said sharply,

"your husband finding out will be the least of your worries."

She gasped and he hung up. Dammit to hell, he believed her. Which got Trey off the hook.

And put them back on the path to viewing Macy's mother as a suspect.

MACY WAS STILL stewing over Esme's cryptic response when Stone returned.

"Trey's alibi checks out," he said. "I guess we have to cut him loose."

Macy sighed, relieved that her ex actually hadn't tried to murder her in cold blood. Although that pointed the finger back at her mother, which would be even more difficult to accept.

"I'll get him," Stone said. He disappeared through the back, and a couple of minutes later, returned with Trey. Belligerence radiated from her ex as he glared at her.

"I told you I was innocent, so stop trying to pin everything bad that happens to you on me," he growled. "Did you ever think that you bring these things on yourself?"

His comment felt like a punch in the gut. Stone gripped his arms and shoved Trey against the wall. "Listen to me, Trey, and listen good. Stay away from Macy. If you so much as make a phone call to her or come within twenty-five feet of her, I'll arrest you for stalking and attempted murder."

Trey raised his chin in challenge. "Good luck making that stick."

"Even if it doesn't," Stone said with a menacing smile, "it'll make your life hell. And I'll enjoy every minute of it."

Trey jerked his arm away from Stone, shot Macy a venomous look, then strode across the room. The door slammed as he exited, the air in the office fraught with tension.

Macy's phone buzzed. The Franceses' number. Her breath quickened. Had Esme decided to talk?

She connected the call. "Special Agent Macy Stark. Esme?"

"No, this is her husband, Buddy." His voice was low, muffled. "She told me about your call, and she doesn't know I'm talking to you. I'd like to keep it that way."

Macy stiffened. "I'm listening."

His uneven breathing filled the silence for a moment. "You wanted to know about the Walkmans?"

"Yes."

"Everything Esme told you is true," Buddy said. "But she had a soft spot for the couple, felt really sorry for them after they lost the boy."

"That was tragic," Macy murmured.

"It was," Buddy agreed. "But after a few months the wife was really depressed and her husband… well, he was having a hard time."

"That's understandable," Macy said, unsure where this was going.

"What I'm trying to say here, and I'm not trying to malign his character, and Esme doesn't want the press to get hold of this, but…well, he tried to seduce Esme."

Macy's breath caught.

"She turned him down, and he put pressure on her, but we were dating and she told me and…so she cut ties."

Now the conversation with Esme made sense. "I see. How did Mr. Walkman handle the rejection?" Macy asked.

"He was miffed, but he offered her a nice severance, and she agreed to keep quiet about it because, like I said, she felt sorry for the couple and didn't want his wife to find out."

The hair on the back of Macy's neck prickled. If Prentice Walkman had been looking for comfort with Esme, he could have looked for it after she left.

Her mother came to work for the couple shortly after Esme left. What if he'd tried to seduce her?

STONE SAW THE discomfort on Macy's face as she ended the call. "What is it?"

Macy tapped her fingers on her arm. "I talked to Esme Frances and her husband. She cleaned for the Walkmans before my mother went to work there."

"I gather that she had something interesting to say about the Walkmans," Stone said gruffly.

Macy nodded, then relayed her conversation with Buddy. "Esme kept quiet to protect the couple out of compassion for their situation."

Stone's jaw tightened. "So while his wife was grieving, he was going to cheat on her with the housekeeper."

Macy didn't like it, either. "A real stand-up guy," she muttered.

"And one who wouldn't have wanted that to come out," Stone said.

"According to Esme's husband," Macy said, "he gave her a nice severance so she would keep quiet."

Stone grunted in disgust, but the jumbled pieces of the puzzling case were shifting, maybe into place. "Are you thinking what I'm thinking?"

Macy raised a brow. "That if he tried to seduce Esme, he might have done the same thing with someone else." Emotions glittered in her eyes. "Like my mother." She swallowed back emotions. "And what if he succeeded? Mom was young and vulnerable and alone. Maybe she gave in. Or…maybe he paid her for sex." The statement felt sour on her tongue, but she couldn't ignore the possibility.

Stone ran his hand through his hair. "He could have paid her to keep quiet."

Macy paled, and he realized where her mind was headed.

"The timing, when my mother worked for the couple…" Macy said, pushing the papers around as she looked at dates. "She went to work for them the year before I was born." She searched another set of papers, frown lines deepening her forehead. "And the house was paid off around my first birthday."

She leaned her head into her hands. "Good God, Stone. We wondered if my real father paid off that loan. What if that man is Prentice Walkman?"

Stone's heart pounded. Walkman was a well-known and respected attorney. He was also running for senate. If he had an illegitimate child, he wouldn't want that to come out now, not with the upcoming election. "Dammit, Macy. I don't like this. We have to talk to the Walkmans."

Macy felt sick to her stomach. Was it possible Prentice Walkman was her father?

All these years she'd wondered…had looked at men on the streets or in stores or restaurants and wondered if he might be right in front of her. If he lived in Briar Ridge.

If he'd kept in touch with her mother.

If he'd known her mother was ill and hadn't cared enough to try to save her.

And now…to think he might be an established attorney, a man running for senate…that he had known and paid her mother to keep his dirty little secret.

"Excuse me." She stood and rushed toward the restroom, a dizzy spell clawing at her. Inside, she closed the door and staggered to the sink, then ran cold water and splashed her face. Nauseated, her hands shook as she snatched a couple of paper towels and dampened them, then pressed them to the back of her neck. Her body was trembling, anger and disbelief making her stomach seize into a hard knot.

A sob wrenched her gut, and for a moment, she allowed the tears to fall before she pulled herself together.

Then a seed of doubt bled through her emotions.

She could be wrong. Could be jumping to conclusions.

Drying her face with another paper towel, she straightened and finger-combed her hair, then exhaled.

Stone was right. They had to question the Walkmans. It wouldn't be an easy conversation, but now that the ugly thought had planted itself in her mind she couldn't let it go without following through.

Her mother had definitely been working for the Walkmans when she was conceived. If Prentice wasn't her father, he and his wife might know who was.

Pinching her cheeks to bring back the color, she tossed the paper towels in the trash, then opened the door. Stone was waiting in the hall, his eyes dark with concern.

"Macy?"

"I'm fine," she said quickly.

He jangled his keys in his hand. "I called and Mrs. Walkman is home. I told her I needed to speak to her and her husband. If you want to stay here, I'll go alone."

Macy shook her head. "I want to see their faces when we confront them."

Stone muttered that he understood, stopped at the reception desk and told Hattie Mae Perkins he'd be out for a while, then they walked outside together.

Macy lapsed into silence as Stone drove them through town. The stores and street signs were decorated for the Fourth with red, white and blue streamers, and flyers advertised the parade and kids' bicycle decorating contest.

Macy faintly remembered the town's celebration when she was younger. Vendors selling handmade crafts and jams and jellies pitched tarps to hawk their wares, and food trucks set up in the town square while the covered pavilion became a stage for local musicians. Bluegrass and country music bands were featured along with cloggers and the kids' dance teams in town performed. American flags hung everywhere, and she saw a group of high schoolers gathered working on the float for the parade.

She tried to remember if her mother had ever brought her to the parade, but the only faces she remembered were Kate's and her mother's. God, she missed that woman.

Halfway to the Walkmans' house, which was miles and miles out of town and near Asheville, Stone stopped at the Barbeque Pit, and they went inside and ordered sandwiches and sweet potato fries. The smoky scent of pulled pork, chicken and brisket filled the quaint restaurant, and Stone dug into his as if he hadn't eaten in days.

Macy nibbled on hers, although she barely tasted the food.

"If Walkman did have an affair, or affairs," Stone said as he licked sauce from his fingers, "I wonder if the wife knew."

Macy's chest clenched with guilt as she thought of the timing and that the woman had just lost her son.

If Mrs. Walkman was unaware of her husband's extramarital activities, Macy was about to blow Adeline's world up again.

THIRTY MINUTES LATER, Stone pulled down a long oak-tree-lined driveway to the Walkman estate, a stately Georgian home with its own tennis courts, pool and pond. An afternoon rain cloud rolled in, casting the property in gray, the balmy temperature outside dropping slightly as a breeze stirred the air.

He took one glance at Macy, though, and knew the scenery was lost on her. He couldn't begin to imagine how she felt.

Together they walked up to the door, and he rang the bell. A woman in a maid's uniform opened the door and greeted them, then showed them to a formal living room with a white sofa, wingback chairs in an ocean-blue color and a stone fireplace that added warmth.

Across the hall, Stone noticed a dark-paneled office that obviously belonged to Mr. Walkman. Odd how different the two spaces were.

Mrs. Walkman looked up from one of the wing chairs as they entered, brushing her hands over the legs of her slacks. Stone introduced them, and Macy forced a smile, although he could feel anxiety radiating from her in waves.

Mrs. Walkman greeted them with a hesitant smile, eyebrow lifted as she spoke. "You made this sound like it was important," she said to Stone. "I called Prentice. He'll be here shortly." She gestured toward the pitcher of iced tea in the center of a tray on the cherry coffee table. "Would you like some tea? Coffee? Water?"

"No, thank you," Stone said. "We just ate lunch."

She turned her attention to Macy and gestured toward the pitcher. "Agent Stark?"

Macy shook her head. "We just want to talk."

"Then sit down." She poured herself a glass of tea, then took a sip. "Is this about my husband's campaign?"

Macy seemed to be staring at the woman in a silent debate over how to proceed. He'd never seen her look so uncertain.

"No, ma'am," Stone said, taking the lead. "I assume you've seen the news about what's going on in Briar Ridge this last week. That the body of a man was found in a house that belongs to a woman named Lynn Stark."

Mrs. Walkman fluttered a diamond-clad hand to her chest, her eyes sparking with some emotion Stone couldn't quite define. "I'm sorry, but I haven't kept up. I've been so busy running my children's nonprofit and campaigning with Prentice that I haven't seen much of the news."

Macy cleared her throat. "We know that Lynn worked for you at one time. And as I told you when I phoned before, I'm her daughter. Do you remember her, Mrs. Walkman?"

The woman's face blanched slightly as if she was uncomfortable, then she gave a tiny nod. "Yes, poor Lynn. It was such a long time ago, and we've had several different housekeepers since over the years." Her voice wavered slightly, and she rubbed the gold locket dangling over her chest between her fingers. "My mind is a blur about that time in our life. We were grieving over my son's death when she worked for us."

"I'm truly sorry about your loss," Macy said.

"So am I," Stone said. "I'm sure it was traumatic."

"You never get over losing a child. Parents are just not supposed to have to bury their children," Mrs. Walkman said, sadness tingeing her voice. "That's the reason I started the nonprofit. It's in Charlie's name. I wanted to help other children who might need help. I couldn't save my son, but at least we help provide grieving families with a support group."

"That's very admirable," Macy said, her expression still torn. "But I'm trying to learn all I can about my mother. She disappeared from the in-house treatment program where she was staying, and it's important I find her."

"Oh, yes, of course dear." The ice in the woman's tea clinked as she lifted her glass. "I wish I could help you, but I haven't talked to or seen Lynn in years."

Stone studied the woman's reaction. She seemed so nice and caring, just as she appeared on-screen.

Macy cleared her throat. "I've reviewed my mother's financials from that time. That's the reason I'm here. The salary you paid her was more than twice what her other employers did, and you even paid her after she left your employ. Can you explain that?"

"Well," Mrs. Walkman said softly. "Your mother was kind to me when I was going through a rough time. I figured she needed some help, so we gave her a few weeks' pay after we moved to help her until she could find more work."

"Mrs. Walkman," Macy said after a minute. "Did

you ever notice my mother and your husband being friendly together?"

Mrs. Walkman curled her fingers around the arms of her chair. "My husband is friendly and nice to everyone. That's his nature."

"But were they ever alone?" Macy pressed.

Anger flared in the other woman's eyes. "Exactly what are you trying to say?"

"I don't mean to be blunt, but I need the truth. Around my first birthday, my mother received a lump cash amount to pay off her mortgage. I have reason to believe that she had an affair with your husband and that he paid her to keep quiet."

The woman's eyes widened in shock, and her glass slipped between her fingers and hit the floor. Glass shattered and tea spilled, trickling all over the pristine wood floor.

## *Chapter Twenty*

Macy studied Mrs. Walkman's reaction, but the usually unflappable woman she'd seen on TV was difficult to read. She obviously was upset by their line of questioning, but was she upset because she'd known her husband had cheated on her and wanted to keep it quiet? Or because she was shocked at the suggestion of an affair?

She and Stone allowed her a moment to process the information, then Mrs. Walkman's expression turned steely. "I don't know where you got our information," she said, a bite to her voice. "Or if you're trying to malign my husband's character because of some secret political agenda, but I can assure you Prentice did not have an affair with that woman."

"Are you certain?" Macy asked. "We understand that you and your husband were having a difficult time back then," she said as gently as possible. "Losing a child often tears couples apart. Maybe he needed comfort elsewhere, and you even forgave him because you were so distraught and grief-stricken yourself."

Perspiration beaded the woman's forehead as she

clenched her hands together in an effort to control her anger. "Yes, we were grief-stricken, but my husband and I love each other, and he would never have stepped out on me."

Suddenly footsteps echoed in the foyer, and a door slammed in the background. A minute later, Prentice Walkman appeared in the doorway, his expression wary as he paused to take in the scene.

"What's going on, honey?" he said to his wife.

The couple exchanged a look, and Mrs. Walkman's shoulders sagged in relief. "Thank God you're here, Prentice. This sheriff and FBI agent…you won't believe what they came here saying."

The senatorial candidate went still, his manicured hand automatically adjusting his red power tie. His eyes darkened, and Macy imagined his lawyer's mind already creating a defensive strategy. The best way to learn the truth was to catch him off guard.

But the idea that he might have slept with her mother, that he might actually be her father, caught *her* off guard. Was she looking at the man who'd gotten her mother pregnant, then abandoned them to preserve his marriage and career?

Stone read the sudden emotions in Macy's silence and understood the reason, so he cleared his throat to give her time to recover. "Mr. Walkman, please sit down. We have some questions for you and your wife."

His rigid posture as he crossed the room made Stone wonder if he knew the reason for their visit. He might be running for senate, but if he was Macy's father and he'd abandoned her years ago and covered it up, he had no respect for the man. Especially knowing how Macy had suffered growing up.

Nothing pissed him off more than a man in power taking advantage of a vulnerable woman.

Walkman sat down beside his wife and clasped her hand in his. "So what is this about?"

Stone explained that they were looking for Lynn Stark and that they knew she'd worked for the couple years ago. He reiterated that they were sorry about the couple's son's death, then he mentioned the payments made to Macy's mother.

"We know Lynn received a large lump sum payment around her daughter's first birthday to pay off her house, and are wondering about your personal relationship to Lynn Stark," Stone said.

Mr. Walkman's expression remained unfazed. "The only relationship my wife and I had with Lynn Stark was as her employer," he said. "And that was not for long. I'm sorry to say your mother was slightly unstable, and then we moved and had no need for her services."

"She became pregnant while she worked for you, didn't she?" Stone asked.

"Yes," Mr. Walkman murmured. "She told us that the father of her baby was dangerous, and that she didn't know how she was going to make ends meet." He squeezed his wife's hand. "Adeline felt sorry for her, so we gave her a nice severance check to hold her over once we moved away." He stood. "Now, we've answered your questions," he said. "I think you should go. Talking about that time brings up painful memories for my wife." His voice softened. "You understand."

He was smooth, Stone thought. Maybe too smooth. "One more thing. Lynn's financial records showed that she received a large cash payment around her daughter's first birthday to pay off her house. What do you know about that?"

"Nothing," Mr. Walkman said. "Maybe she had family who stepped up. Or maybe she lied about the baby's father, and he decided to help her out."

"You see, that's exactly what we're thinking," Stone said. "That the father may have paid her to keep his identity quiet."

"I wish I could tell you more," Mr. Walkman said. "But I can't."

Macy folded her arms. "I suspect you can."

He angled his head toward her, his green eyes piercing Macy's. "Excuse me?"

Macy lifted her chin. "Did you have an affair with my mother?"

MACY HELD HER breath as she waited on Walkman's response. For a fraction of a second, surprise, then a sliver of anger appeared before his eyes softened.

"I'm sorry, Agent Stark, I can see that you're looking for answers and grasping, but the answer is no." He patted his wife's hand, and she gave him a doting smile. "I love my wife and always have. I would never be unfaithful."

Macy remembered Esme's statement, more specifically her husband's, and knew he was lying. But she refused to throw Esme under the bus for fear he might retaliate against the woman. She'd stepped away from his employ out of respect for herself, her husband and Mr. Walkman's wife.

Macy raised a brow. "Then if I asked other housekeepers who've worked for you over the years, they will confirm that your relationship with them has always been aboveboard?"

"Absolutely," Mr. Walkman said.

"I can assure you that our marriage is solid now and always has been," Mrs. Walkman said.

"Then you won't mind providing me with a list of your other housekeepers over the years?" Macy said with an eyebrow raise.

The couple exchanged looks. "I'm afraid not," Mr. Walkman said. "For all I know, you want to smear my campaign. But you have no right to invade people's privacy because you're on a witch hunt to malign me."

Macy gave him a deadpan look. "If you've been faithful as you say, you have nothing to worry about."

A muscle ticked in Mr. Walkman's jaw. "Unless you have a warrant, I don't intend to open up my private life for you to dissect," Mr. Walkman said. "We're done here. If you have more questions, I'd prefer to have my attorney present."

Macy gritted her teeth. She just bet he would.

Stone stood. "Thanks for your time. If you think of anything else that might help us, maybe where Lynn Stark would go or someone she might turn to for help, please give me a call."

"We haven't heard from that woman or seen her in over two decades," Mr. Walkman said. "So we have no idea where she is or where she'd go."

Macy forced an even expression. "One more question, Mr. and Mrs. Walkman. Did either of you know a man named Voight Hubert?"

Mrs. Walkman's eyes narrowed, and she shook her head. Her husband's mouth tightened into a thin line. "No. Who is he?"

"He was an ex-con," Macy said, still gauging their reactions. "He was also the man found murdered at my mother's house." Macy glanced at the husband. "Are you sure you don't recognize the name? Maybe through your law practice at some time."

"I'm quite certain I don't." Walkman stood, adjusting his tie. Dismissing them.

Mrs. Walkman offered Macy a sympathetic smile. "It must have been difficult growing up with an unstable mother. I hope you find what you're looking for, dear."

Macy's gaze met hers. The woman's tone sounded sincere, yet the dig about her mother hurt. "All I'm looking for is the truth," she said frankly. "And I won't stop looking until I find it."

She noticed the woman lean into her husband, and Macy almost felt sorry for her. But as she and Stone walked through the marble-floored foyer, she pushed her sympathy aside. The couple's relationship was not as picture-perfect as it appeared. Photographs and news interviews in the media painted false portraits of happiness and bliss all the time.

Esme and her husband told a different story.

Disturbing thoughts congregated in her mind as she slid into Stone's police car.

"I think they're lying," Stone said as he veered onto the main highway leading back toward town.

"Yes," Macy agreed. "The question is to what extent." Different scenarios played through her mind. "If Walkman slept with my mother and his wife found out, she could have been angry with my mother. Or under the duress of her grief, she could have forgiven him, and they reconciled."

"We have to determine if that lump cash payout came from them," Stone said, his jaw clenched. "But I don't think we have enough for a judge to issue a warrant or to subpoena their financials."

"Or to obtain a sample of his DNA." Macy twisted her mouth in thought. She knew a guy at the Bureau who could do a little hacking into the financials. But obtaining a DNA sample without Walkman's permission would be even trickier.

Her mind began to sort through all they knew. "We can't forget that the dead man in the wall at my house was a hit man. As an attorney, Prentice Walkman would have had access to contacts or criminals who connected him to Hubert."

"Good point," Stone said.

Macy nodded. "He could have hired Hubert to kill my mother so she couldn't expose his dirty little secret." Her lungs strained for air.

That dirty little secret was her.

STONE CLENCHED THE steering wheel. The Walkmans' house was beautiful, the house ornate, the couple inside a portrait of marital bliss, devotion and longevity.

But he sensed something was off. That Mrs. Walkman had intentionally made the comment about Macy's mother to rile her. Or to imply that Macy might be unstable herself.

Had she known about her husband's philandering and turned a blind eye for the sake of their marriage and his career? Had he slept with women other than Lynn Stark?

Then the more disturbing question, one he knew was haunting Macy. Was he Macy's father?

"About the DNA," Stone said. "Walkman was in the military years ago. The armed forces maintains a DNA reference specimen collection in an automated database to assist in identifying human remains."

"You're right." Macy pulled her phone from her pocket, punched in a number and called her FBI boss. "I know this is dancing the line, but I need your help." She explained her theory about Walkman and that she wanted his DNA compared to her own." Tension stretched for a moment while she listened to his response. "Okay, thanks;"

"He's going to do it?" Stone asked, impressed as she ended the call.

"As a favor to me," Macy said.

A smile twitched at Stone's mouth at her comment, but the seriousness of the situation quickly forced it away.

They needed proof against Walkman. Making accusations without evidence could ruin his career. And if they were wrong, it would compromise both of their jobs.

But if they were right and Walkman had hired Hubert to kill Lynn Stark, then Macy's father might be a killer.

NIGHT HAD FALLEN by the time Macy and Stone arrived back in Briar Ridge. The sun had faded, a slight breeze stirring the humid air as rain clouds moved across the sky, rumbling with the promise of a summer storm.

Stone drove to his cabin, and Macy shivered as they went inside. She kept replaying the possibility that Walkman was her father. Was he capable of having someone murder her mother?

If he was, he was a monster…

Macy set her laptop up and so did Stone, then he set out the dinners they'd picked up on the pine table.

"I have a PI named Delwood I work with sometimes," she told Stone. "Let me call him. He might be able to help."

Stone nodded, and she stepped onto the back deck and called him. He had expert hacking skills. They might not be able to use what he found in court if he crossed the line, but she could use it as a lead to find the truth or pressure the Walkmans to talk. "It's Agent Stark. I need you to do something for me and to keep it confidential."

"Only way I work," Delwood said.

Macy chuckled. If he didn't, he'd go to jail. She didn't like stepping into the gray areas, but sometimes it was the fastest way to get things done. "I need whatever you can find financial-wise on Prentice Walkman," Macy said.

"What?" Delwood rarely reacted. "You mean *the* Prentice Walkman running for senate?"

"Yes," Macy said. "I'm interested in going back about twenty-seven, twenty-eight years ago. Look for any large cash withdrawals or payouts, especially to women."

A tense second passed. "Exactly what are you looking for?"

Macy chewed the inside of her cheek. "I think he had an affair, maybe more than one, and may have paid the women to keep quiet." She hesitated. "Also look for any connection, a payout, to a hit man named Voight Hubert. He served time in prison."

Delwood whistled. "You out to get this guy or just ruin his campaign?"

"I don't give a damn about his campaign, although that's why I called you. This has to be handled with discretion. I don't want to malign his character if he is who he claims to be." Although she already knew different. "Understand?"

"Understood. This case must be important."

More important than he knew. Her life depended on uncovering the truth. "It is," Macy said with a shudder as she remembered the fire at her mother's house.

She thanked him, then hung up and went to join Stone. He was on the phone.

"All right, I understand." He hung up and raked a hand through his hair. "I tried to get a warrant, but the judge refused."

Macy nodded. "I'm not surprised. Walkman is high profile."

Macy clenched her hands by her side and sank into the chair. Soon she would know if Prentice Walkman was her father.

All the more reason to dig deep and find out if he was also a killer.

# *Chapter Twenty-One*

Stone scarfed down the pot roast dinner special while he dug through records in search of the attorney who'd represented Hubert years ago. Meanwhile, Macy ate chicken potpie and looked for articles about Prentice Walkman and his wife.

It took a while, but he finally found the information he was seeking. Hubert was represented by a public defender named Willie Robard. The prosecutor was a man named Damon Huntington. There was no mention of Prentice Walkman as his attorney. Although with his law contacts and access to databases, Walkman could have easily accessed Hubert's list of priors and met with him in private. With his job, he would also know not to leave a paper trail.

Next, he searched for cases Walkman had represented dating back twenty-seven years. Like many attorneys, he'd started out as a public defender. But he'd obviously been young and ambitious and quickly moved to a law firm called Bartles & Cohen. A search in public records at the courthouse in the county gave him a list of cases he'd represented that went to court. Again, Hubert was not among them.

On a hunch, though, he decided to call Bubba Yates, Hubert's former prison cellmate. The man didn't answer, so Stone left a message asking him to return his call.

Macy looked up from her laptop. "So far, I haven't found anything except praise for Walkman's skills as a litigator." She rubbed her forehead. "He married his college sweetheart who was a paralegal for a while, then she stayed home with their son when he was born." Sympathy flashed in her eyes. "There's a story here about the accident. So sad."

Stone nodded. To lose a child would be the worst kind of horrible.

Could a grieving mother possibly understand her husband turning to another woman for comfort? Or would she see that as the ultimate betrayal?

"Walkman worked a couple of high-profile cases involving gangs about ten years ago. I couldn't find any articles dating back twenty-five, twenty-seven years ago. He was young, so those cases were probably small and not newsworthy."

Stone's phone buzzed. "Sheriff Lawson."

"It's Bubba Yates."

"Yes, thank you for returning my call. I had another question for you." Stone drummed his fingers on the table. "What was the name of the attorney who represented you when your case went to trial?"

Yates sighed. "His name was Walkman. He's big now, saw him on the news running for senate."

Stone's stomach clenched as he hung up. "Macy," he said. "I just found the connection between Walkman and Hubert."

"What is it?" Macy asked.

"Walkman worked as a public defender when he first started practicing law. Although he didn't represent Hubert, he did represent Hubert's cellmate Bubba Yates."

Macy's heart stuttered. "Then he could have met him or known about him through Yates."

"Exactly. Yates was quick to tell us how mean Hubert was. He probably would have told his attorney, too."

Macy nodded, her earlier headache returning. Her eyes were gritty from studying the computer files, her head spinning with her encounter with the Walkmans.

The entire time she'd sat in his living room, she'd studied the man, searching for some sign that he was her father, that she had his nose or mouth or jawline or some tiny feature. That he'd known and kept it secret. That he would have tried to hurt her mother.

That he hadn't just lied to her face.

But he was cool as a cucumber under pressure. That quality alone made for a good litigator and politician.

It also meant he'd want to protect that reputation.

She scrolled through photos of Walkman from the media. He was a handsome-looking man. Neat and well groomed. A charming smile. Narrow face. A slight cleft in his chin. Eyes that twinkled when he smiled.

Again she searched for herself in his face and those eyes, but saw no resemblance.

She went back years in her search and finally found a photo of him when he was a public defender. He was young, midtwenties. She could easily see why her mother might have been tempted to sleep with him.

The article about his son's death made her chest squeeze. The couple stood huddled together, the wife's head buried against his chest as she sobbed at the funeral. Walkman's own expression looked tortured.

Had her mother felt so sorry for him that she'd ignored the fact that he was married and crawled in his bed to comfort him?

The next few weeks, there were more articles and photographs. The couple had started a charity in their son's name and held a fundraiser. In those photos, though, the couple's grief seemed to have grown even more intense, the stage of grief playing out. Shock, denial, anger, anguish.

No longer was Mrs. Walkman leaning into her husband. In fact, they stood a foot apart on stage as they addressed the guests.

Another candid shot showed Walkman smiling down at one of the servers. Something about his eyes suggested he knew her. Maybe intimately.

Macy stood and stretched. If he had had multiple affairs, how had his wife not known?

She might have forgiven one, but more than one? How did a woman live with that kind of betrayal?

STONE COULDN'T IMAGINE how Macy was feeling, but at least tonight he knew she was safe. She walked over to the fireplace and seemed to be studying the river rocks on his mantel.

"I need to talk to the Walkmans again," Macy said as she picked up a stone and ran her finger over the slick surface.

"Of course." He walked up behind her and rubbed her arms. "But not tonight. It's storming. You need to rest."

She shivered as thunder boomed outside, then gave a little nod and set the rock back on the mantel. "You collect river rocks?"

He rolled his shoulders, emotions hitting him. "My mom loved them. She named me Stone after the smooth river rocks she found when we went camping. She used to paint messages on them and leave them around town."

Macy turned to him with an odd look in her eyes. "Oh my God, Stone. I used to collect those. The messages she wrote on them inspired me to have hope."

Stone's throat clogged with emotions. Macy had never met his mother, but somehow knowing she had collected his mother's rocks touched him deeply. "She was special," he murmured.

"She was." Macy looked away, then rubbed her arms as if to ward off a chill. Stone took out the bottle of whiskey he kept in the cabinet and poured them both a small tumbler. Macy stared at it for a moment, then accepted the glass and sipped.

He tossed back the shot, savoring the warm burn of alcohol as it slid down his throat. His gaze met hers, and temptation rolled through him. Macy was tough and strong and even more beautiful because of it. He wanted to alleviate all her worries.

Macy turned her glass up and finished the whiskey, then ran a hand through her hair. "I'm tired. I think you're right. I need to get some rest."

Concern for Macy made him want to reach for her. But before he could, she grabbed her phone and disappeared into the bedroom. Stone wanted to go after her and hold her, but he sensed she needed time to process what was going on, so he let her go.

He poured himself another shot, then went to the sliding glass doors and looked out at the storm as it raged through the sky. Lightning zigzagged across the treetops, thunder rumbling as the rain began to pour and beat at the house.

He scanned the yard for an intruder, then checked the locks on the sliders and the front door. Then he set his alarm.

If Walkman was guilty and had hired Hubert years ago, he might be panicked now that they'd questioned him. Who was to say that he might not hire someone else to come after Macy?

MACY JUMPED AS the storm thundered outside. Lightning illuminated the mountain peaks, and she rushed to the window and looked out. The jagged lines of the trees resembled monsters clawing at her, just as they had when she was a child.

Fear seized her, making it hard to breathe, and she quickly closed the curtains, then crawled beneath the covers and pulled them up over her head.

The rain pummeling the roof sounded like nails hammering tin and sent a shiver through her.

She pressed her fist to her mouth to stifle a sob and closed her eyes, but the storm transported her back in time. She was five again, hiding in the dark, terrified of the thunder and lightning.

Finally, it quieted enough for her to fall asleep, but sometime later thunder startled her awake. Then she heard the voices.

*A woman...her mother screaming. Something being thrown. Furniture overturned. Another woman's voice? No...a man's. Deep, sinister. Footsteps.*

*Another scream. Her mother crying...*

*She slipped from bed, tiptoed to the door and peeked through the opening. It was so dark she could barely see. A shadow...a man. Lightning shot across the hallway, then a shadow moved. Her mother was screaming and kicking again. The man hit her and she flew across the room and smacked the wall.*

*Cold terror gripped Macy, and she couldn't move.*

*"No!" her mother screamed. She tried to get up, but the man turned and punched her again, then he stalked toward Macy's room.*

*"Run, Macy! Run!" her mother cried.*

*Macy finally made her legs move and ran back toward her bed. She crawled underneath it, trembling as she hid her face in her hands. She heard the door screech open. Peered between her fingers and saw the man's shoes...coming closer.*

*Then her mother screamed again and lunged at the man.*

"Macy!"

Stone's voice dragged her from the memory, and she heard him walking toward her. Slowly, she lowered the covers to make certain it was him.

The bed dipped as he sat down beside her, and his fingers gently brushed her cheek. "Are you okay? I heard you screaming."

She hadn't realized she'd screamed out loud. He wiped her tears with his finger, and she had to swallow twice to make her voice work. "Nightmare."

His dark gaze raked over her. "Want to talk about it?"

She sat up and pushed her tangled hair from her face. "It was about that night. I… The man was in my house. I think it was Hubert."

He breathed out. "You saw him?"

"Not his face, but a man. My mother was screaming, and he was coming toward my room, but she tried to stop him."

"He was coming into your room?" he asked gruffly.

Macy nodded, a shudder ripping through her. "My mother yelled at me to run, but there was nowhere to go, so I hid under the bed."

Stone muttered a curse. "He came to kill your mother and he was going to take you."

"Or kill me," Macy said in a strangled voice.

STONE CLENCHED HIS jaw so tight he thought it would break. Dammit. Would Walkman have ordered his own daughter to be murdered?

Anger hardened his tone. "If Walkman is responsible for all of this, he's going to pay."

Macy clutched his hand. Another boom of thunder roared, and she startled, her breath gushing out. He couldn't resist. He pulled her into his arms and rubbed her back. She pressed her head against his chest and clung to him, trembling in his arms.

"It's all right," he murmured. "You're safe tonight." And he'd keep her that way if she'd let him.

He held her for what seemed like forever, stroking her hair and back. Her breathing grew more steady, then she lifted her head and looked into his eyes. Their gazes locked, heat sizzling between them. Desire bolted through him, and he lifted his fingers and brushed her cheek again.

She licked her lips and cupped his face between her hands. "Thank you for being here, Stone."

His heart pounded. He told himself to walk away, but Macy pulled his face toward her and pressed her mouth to his, and he lost his will and kissed her. One taste and he wanted more. She moved her lips against his in a sensual rhythm that tied his belly in knots, and he deepened the kiss. Need and desire blazed through him, but he forced himself to pause and looked into her eyes.

"I don't want to take advantage of you," he murmured.

A smile sparkled in her eyes, the most beautiful thing he'd ever seen. Then she traced her finger over his lips, and his body hardened. He sucked her finger into his mouth, and she drew him to her again.

Their lips melded together, tongues dancing, and

he wrapped his arms around her. She leaned into him, then tugged at the top button of his shirt. His breath stalled as she unfastened the buttons, and she pressed a kiss to his chest.

He lowered his head and nibbled at her neck, tugging at the strap to her tank top. Another kiss and another, then they tore at each other's clothes. His shirt hit the floor along with his jeans, and he lifted her tank top over her head, exposing her generous breasts.

He paused to study her smooth skin and cupped her breasts in his hands. Her breathing grew more erratic, and she raked her hand across his chest and slid it lower to stroke his hard length.

"Macy?" he whispered. "Are you sure?"

She flipped him to his back, then climbed above him and straddled him. Her long hair brushed his chest as she kissed him again, and he pushed at her pajama shorts, stripping her naked and cupping her butt in his hands.

She groaned and removed his boxers, then they deepened the kiss, and she impaled herself on him. He groaned and gripped her hips, their breathing mingling as the tension built and she rode him into oblivion.

# *Chapter Twenty-Two*

The next morning when Stone rolled over, he studied Macy's sleeping form. For once, she seemed actually at peace.

They'd made love again in the night, then she'd curled in his arms. She was sleeping so soundly he decided not to wake her, but he slipped from bed, showered and brewed a pot of coffee. He called his brother, and the phone rang and rang but Mickey didn't answer, so he scribbled Macy a note that he had a quick errand to run.

*Stay put and have some coffee and breakfast*, he wrote. *I'll be back in half an hour.*

He set out a mug, pulled some cinnamon rolls from the pantry and put them on a plate for her, grabbed his keys.

He hated to leave Macy alone, but he was worried sick about his brother. And he needed to get his head on straight about Macy.

He was supposed to be finding the person who wanted her dead, not falling in love with her.

The thought made him jerk to a halt, and he

glanced back at the closed bedroom door. *Was* he in love with Macy?

The thought sobered him. He needed some distance. As soon as they solved this case, Macy would leave Briar Ridge.

And he could never leave, not with Mickey here.

He grabbed his holster and weapon, set the house alarm, then stepped outside. Instincts on alert, he surveyed his property as he walked to his car to make sure no one was lurking around or had followed them.

No one knew Macy was here, he reminded himself. She would be fine until he returned.

Still, his nerves were on edge as he drove toward Mickey's. A light sprinkling of rain began and a thin fog had developed, blurring the trees as he rounded the curvy mountain road. He wound toward town, then veered onto the turn to Mickey's, scanning the streets as he went in case of trouble. Two more days until the Fourth of July parade.

When he reached Mickey's, he hurried up to the door and knocked. Tapping his foot, he waited a couple of minutes, then shouted through the door as he pounded on it. "Mickey, open up!"

He glanced at the window. It was dark inside, but then again, Mickey rarely turned on a light.

"Mickey!" He jiggled the door and was just about to pull out his key when he heard footsteps shuffling inside. Finally, the door opened.

"What is it now?" Mickey growled.

Stone shifted. "You didn't answer the phone when I called."

"I'm busy." Mickey tunneled his fingers through his shaggy hair. He wore a T-shirt and jeans, and he hadn't shaved in days.

"Busy doing what?" Stone asked.

Mickey gripped the door edge to keep Stone from entering. "I've got company," he muttered. "Now go back to your life and let me live mine."

Stone gritted his teeth. "Why are you so pissed at me?"

"Because you treat me like a kid," Mickey said. "Now I really do have company. Go home." He shut the door in Stone's face.

Stone clenched his hands into fists and backed away from the door. He wondered who was in Mickey's place. He sure hadn't wanted Stone to come inside.

Because he didn't want him to know who was in there? If not, why?

MACY WOKE UP to find the bed empty. She could still feel the warm imprint of Stone's body on the pillow and smell his masculine aftershave. Last night had been…incredible. The storm had upset her and triggered her memories, but Stone had helped her forget.

At least for a little while.

But today was a new day. Back to reality.

She couldn't shake the feeling that Mrs. Walkman had known about her husband's affair…or affairs.

Her phone buzzed. Delwood.

"Hey, Macy, I may have found something."

"What is it?"

"The Walkmans had a separate account under the name Maids, Inc. I found several large withdrawals in cash ranging from twenty-five thousand to seventy-five thou."

Seventy thousand was what her mother had received to pay off her house when Macy was one. Instead of Mr. Walkman bribing her mother and the other women he slept with to keep them quiet, Mrs. Walkman might have been the one to pay them.

"Can you tell who opened the account?"

"Mr. Walkman," Delwood said. "Does that help?"

"Yes. Let me know if you find anything else." She hung up and paced over to the window and looked out into the woods. Although the sun was fighting to break through the trees, a light rain drizzled down, a reminder of the night her mother threw her outside.

The night everything changed.

Prentice Walkman might not admit the truth, but somehow she had to reach his wife. Find out if she knew about the payments. Maybe if she talked to her alone…

She quickly dragged on clothes, then hurried to the kitchen. Stone had left a note with coffee so she poured a mug and nibbled on one of the cinnamon rolls. He still hadn't returned, and she was too antsy to sleep. He'd driven his squad car, so she made a snap decision to borrow his pick-up truck to retrieve her car.

Deciding Mrs. Walkman might open up more if she had a woman-to-woman conversation with her, she called and asked her to meet her at a coffee shop named the Brew Pot. The woman reluctantly agreed, and Macy gave her the address.

Maybe without her husband's presence, she'd convince the woman to talk.

LYNN STARK PACED the woods behind the house. She wanted so badly to tell Macy the truth. Tell her everything. But she would never believe her. No one would.

She was a nobody with depression issues. Taking medication for bipolar disorder would not work in her favor. Everyone would say she was crazy.

And she had gone crazy a while back.

Seeing Macy back at the house had done something to her, though. Watching the house where she'd raised her daughter lit on fire…hovering in the shadows while sirens screeched…that sheriff running in and carrying Macy out…

If Macy kept digging, she would find the truth. Then she'd send her to jail. She couldn't be locked up in a damn cage. She'd die in there.

She had to stop Macy.

She patted the gun in her pocket, then pulled the burner phone she'd bought from her pocket and made a call.

THE RAIN SLOWED Macy's drive, but she got her car, and made her way to the Brew Pot. Stone probably wouldn't be pleased that she'd gone without him, but she could take care of herself.

She planned her strategy as she drove, but when she pulled into the Brew Pot's parking lot, she saw

Mrs. Walkman rushing from inside the coffee shop to her car. She looked all around her as if she thought someone was watching her, her eyes panicked as she jumped into her sedan and sped off. Rainwater spewed from the back of her car, and her tires squealed as she cut the steering wheel too fast.

The woman was obviously in a hurry to leave. Why? She'd agreed to the meeting. Where was she going?

Macy followed her, careful to stay a car length behind so the woman wouldn't see her. After several miles, Mrs. Walkman veered off the main highway onto a winding road that led toward some mountain cabins. The area was remote, the woods swallowing her as she maneuvered the narrow road.

Occasionally they passed another car, and twice Macy slowed and allowed a car in front of her to keep Mrs. Walkman from spotting her. They passed several cabins set half a mile apart, then she turned onto a graveled road that wound up a hill.

Macy swerved into a drive and waited a few minutes, then pulled back and started up the road again, which led to a driveway and a cabin set on the hill surrounded by oaks and pines.

She parked on the side of the road beneath a cluster of trees, cut the lights, then slid from the truck. As quietly as she could, she climbed the hill, taking cover between the trees as she went. A few hundred feet and she spotted Mrs. Walkman's sedan parked in front of a large rustic-looking cabin surrounded by trees. Flowers grew in beds along the front, and a wraparound porch ran the length and sides of the house.

Macy froze, remaining still as her gaze scanned the yard for signs of the woman. Inside, she saw a light flip on, and then a shadow appeared in the window. Holding her breath, Macy moved closer, carefully staying beneath the overhang of the tree branches as she inched to the side of the house and crept up on the porch. She had practice in treading quietly and was relieved the structure was newer and the flooring didn't creak.

A noise sounded from the inside, then she heard voices. Mrs. Walkman's. Then another woman's.

Macy went still again, then inched her head up to see through the window.

Shock stole her breath. The other woman was her mother. And she was aiming a gun at Mrs. Walkman.

STONE WAS NOT only worried about Mickey, but angry as hell. Growing up, they'd been so close. Like most boys, they'd tumbled and wrestled in the grass, hiked and fished with their father, and played sports. Stone's had been football, whereas Mickey played baseball. He was also the artistic one and once had dreams of writing music and starting a band.

All those dreams seemed to have died when he became impaired. Although for a short time, he'd rallied and worked for that video game company, creating sound effects and background music. But Stone knew Mickey's heart wasn't in the work.

His heart wasn't in anything anymore.

Frustrated, he drove back to his house, the wet roads and drizzling rain making the asphalt slippery and the visibility foggy. He passed a fender bender, but his deputy was already on the scene handling things, so he hurried on.

By the time he reached his house, he was anxious to see Macy. But when he turned up his drive, he noticed his pickup truck was gone.

A frisson of alarm shot through him. He swung the squad car into Park, then hit the ground running. As soon as he went inside, he knew Macy wasn't there. A hollow emptiness rang through the house as he called her name. An emptiness that made him miss her already.

Still, he raced through the house, shouting her name. Her luggage was still in the guest room. The tangled sheets taunted him with a reminder of the night they'd shared together.

He hoped it wouldn't be the last.

Inhaling a deep breath, he noted her weapon was gone and there was no sign of foul play. He raced back to the kitchen and found the note he'd written to her. Below his scribbled message, she'd written her own.

*Gone to meet Mrs. Walkman at the Brew Pot for a woman-to-woman chat.*

She left the name of the coffee shop for him. Thank God.

He snatched his phone and pressed her number. The phone rang once, then went straight to voicemail. "Call me, Macy. I'll meet you at the Brew Pot."

Furious that she'd left instead of staying safely at his home, he hurried back outside to his squad car. His tires squealed, water and gravel spewing as he sped away. He called Macy several more times as he drove, each minute that passed intensifying his anxiety.

Dammit, she shouldn't have gone off alone. Why hadn't she waited on him?

Because he'd crossed the line and slept with her?

Didn't she trust him by now?

The rain continued to fall as he wound around the mountain. By the time he reached the coffee shop, every muscle in his body screamed with worry. When he swerved into the parking lot, he didn't see his pickup truck. She might have swung by and gotten her own car but it wasn't there either and neither was Mrs. Walkman's.

He checked the tracker on Macy's phone and confirmed she was not at the coffee shop. The GPS coordinates were for a place in the mountains a few miles away.

He flipped on his siren, then sped from the parking lot. Dammit, where was she going? Was she alone or with Mrs. Walkman?

Fear clawed at him. If she knew they were close to unraveling the truth, Macy might be walking into a trap.

MACY STARED IN shock at her mother. She looked wild-eyed, her muddy brown hair a tangled mess around her pale face, the gun bobbing up and down in her trembling hand.

Dear God, she was going to kill Mrs. Walkman.

Macy inched to the door, eased it open, then pulled her service weapon and gripped it at the ready as she crept inside.

The women were screaming at each other, so she activated the recorder on her phone.

"You screwed my husband, you little whore," Mrs. Walkman shouted. "And now your bastard child is trying to ruin my life and Prentice's."

The gun wavered as Macy's mother cried, "I didn't seduce your husband. He pressured me into having sex."

"We were grieving for our son, and you took advantage," Mrs. Walkman shouted. "First you met him at those empty cabins you cleaned. I guess you thought I was a fool and didn't know but I followed him." Her angry breath heaved out. "Then you came here, to my own family's place, like it was some little hideaway of your own." She slid her hand in her pocket and pulled out a .38. "Then you had the audacity to get pregnant. I know you were going to trap my husband into leaving me so he could shack up with you and that illegitimate baby."

Tears streamed down Macy's mother's face. "No, I wasn't. I wanted to get away from him. He was the one who chased after me."

"You're lying!" Mrs. Walkman screamed.

"I wasn't the first one," Macy's mother said. "And I probably wasn't the last."

"You should have left us alone like I warned you to," Mrs. Walkman said in a shrill tone.

"You're insane," Lynn said. "You gaslighted me.

You took Macy from the park that day. I went crazy looking for her, and all the time you had her."

Macy struggled to recall the incident. Tidbits of the memory returned in quick flashes. A woman, getting in her car to see a puppy, them going for a drive. Then the woman pushing her out of the car in front of her house. Her mother screaming and crying hysterically, slamming her fist on the car.

"That was a warning," Mrs. Walkman snarled. "But you didn't listen."

Her mother paced across the room, waving the gun wildly. "So you sent that man to my house. He broke in and tried to kill me. And he was going to kill my daughter, too."

Macy gasped. Had Mrs. Walkman hired the hit man?

She didn't know what to believe. Knowing she needed to defuse the situation, though, she stepped from the shadows of the doorway. Her mother jerked her head up, crazed eyes widening in shock.

Mrs. Walkman swung toward her, the gun bobbing up and down. "You...you're ruining everything!"

Macy lifted her hand in defiance. "It's true, isn't it? I remember the man fighting with my mother in the hall. He knocked her down, then came into my room and was going to take me, but then..." She turned to her mother. "You tackled him."

Her mother's face crumpled, her voice a raw whisper. "I grabbed the kitchen knife. I had to protect you, Macy."

"He tried to get the knife, but you stabbed him

over and over and over," Macy said, the image of the blood spattering haunting her.

"I'm sorry, Macy…" she cried. "I had to save you. But then… I got scared that no one would believe me." She gestured to Mrs. Walkman. "Prentice was an attorney. He had connections. I thought he sent the man and if I'd called the police, he would have lied and then I would have gone to prison, and you would have ended up in the system."

Tears blurred Macy's vision. "But you threw me out in the rain."

"I had to get you out of the house. I didn't want you seeing all that blood," Lynn cried. "And I had to get rid of the body."

"So you put him in the wall," Macy said. And then her mother had had a psychotic break. "I thought you didn't love me," Macy said. "That you wanted to get rid of me."

A sob escaped Lynn. "No, but I…was traumatized after that. Every time I closed my eyes, I saw that man trying to take you, saw all that blood. It was gurgling from his throat and running all over the place. Then his body jerked and his eyes went blank and…" She aimed the gun at Mrs. Walkman's chest. "You lost your son, but you were going to have my daughter killed. How could any mother do that?"

"Don't expect me to feel sorry for you," Mrs. Walkman snarled. "Prentice promised to take care of you once and for all. He thought money would do it, but I knew you'd just keep coming back for more. I had to be the one to get rid of you." Fury filled Mrs. Walkman's face as she whipped the gun up and fired at Lynn.

Macy lunged toward her to grab the gun, but her mother fell to the floor, blood gushing from her stomach. Then Mrs. Walkman turned the gun on Macy.

But Macy fired her own weapon and the bullet pierced the woman in the chest. The impact flung her backward against the wall, blood spurting, then she sank to the floor, body convulsing.

# *Chapter Twenty-Three*

Stone heard the gunshots, pulled his weapon and stormed into the cabin. Mrs. Walkman was lying on the floor, eyes staring wide open in shock, blood dribbling from her mouth. Macy was kneeling beside her mother, blood soaking her hands and clothing.

Fear pounded inside him. “Macy?”

She angled her head toward him, and he realized her mother was shot and Macy was trying to stop the bleeding with her hands.

“Call 911!” she yelled.

He rushed to Mrs. Walkman, kicked her gun away and checked for a pulse. But it was too late. She was dead.

Stowing his gun in his holster, he pulled his phone and called for an ambulance. Then he hurried over to Macy and her mother.

“Are you hit?” he asked Macy.

She shook her head no.

“What happened?” Stone asked.

“She was trying to protect me like she did years ago,” Macy said. “I remember Hubert breaking in.

Mrs. Walkman hired him to kill us both." A tear trickled down her cheek. "I got it all on tape."

Stone swallowed back the horror, then squeezed her arm, ran to the kitchen and grabbed a handful of kitchen towels from a drawer. He carried them back to her to use as blood stoppers, then called a crime scene unit to process the house.

The next hour was pure chaos as the ambulance arrived. Lynn was going to make it but needed surgery to remove the bullet from her stomach.

"I'm going to arrest Walkman," Stone said. "Even if his wife ordered the hit, he was an accomplice."

Macy nodded, thanked him, then climbed into the ambulance with her mother. His heart ached for her and for the years they'd lost. She'd grown up thinking her mother didn't love her.

Instead, her mother had loved her so much she'd killed to protect her.

But her father… Now she knew his name. That he hadn't wanted her.

That his wife had tried to kill her and her mother.

How could she live with that?

TWO HOURS LATER, Macy kissed her mother's cheek and went to meet Stone in the waiting room for an update. She had a feeling the shock would set in at some point, but for now she was grateful her mother had survived surgery and that she was going to be all right. At least physically.

She still had to deal with the emotional trauma, but during the ambulance ride, her mother promised she'd return to the inpatient program and do whatever it took to get better.

Macy believed her. Even the psychiatrist she'd spoken with while her mother underwent surgery seemed hopeful that now that Lynn had faced and confronted the past, she might be able to recover and move on.

Was it possible that she could have a relationship with her mother now? That the two of them could be friends, even?

Stone strode into the waiting room, his big body tense. Gretta Wright rushed in behind him, took a look at Macy, whose clothes were still stained in blood, and gaped at her.

"Oh my God," she muttered.

"Do not put your camera on Macy," Stone hissed.

Gretta shook her head. "No, I won't. But I want an exclusive. I heard that you arrested Prentice Walkman and that his wife is dead."

Macy gritted her teeth. "Tomorrow we'll do a press conference and go over everything. But not tonight."

For once, Gretta didn't argue. She accepted the deal and turned and left.

Stone walked over to her, his look of concern touching a place deep inside her, stirring more emotions. "How are you holding up?"

"Okay." Although she wasn't okay and they both knew it.

But she would be. She was tough. Resilient. She had friends, Kate and Brynn. Her mother had loved her.

And Stone was here.

But she couldn't voice those feelings right now. "The doctors gave my mom a good prognosis. She's agreed to go back to the psychiatric facility for treatment."

"That's good news," he agreed.

Macy's stomach twisted with worry. "She did kill Hubert and hide him in the wall," Macy said. "Do you plan to charge her?"

Stone's gaze met hers. "She obviously killed him in self-defense. Her real crime was covering it up."

"Because she was afraid," Macy said. "She was protecting me."

Stone brushed a strand of hair from her cheek. "I understand that. And I think a judge will, too."

Macy wanted to kiss him. But she was a bloody mess, and Kate and Brynn rushed in, looking frantic as they hurried to her.

"I'll need to confront Prentice Walkman," she told Stone.

Stone nodded. "Not yet. He's already lawyered up. Tonight just clean up and rest." He offered Kate and Brynn an encouraging smile as they approached. "And be with your friends."

She gave a little nod, although she wanted to ask him to stay with her. To make love to her again.

But Macy didn't ask for things. And soon she would need to leave. No need to think that Stone had been doing anything the night before except comforting her because he was such a caring man.

She needed to pack in the morning. She could come back and visit her mother when she wanted. But her life wasn't here anymore.

# *Chapter Twenty-Four*

*One week later*

Macy packed her suitcase with mixed emotions and dragged her bag to the car. She'd come to Briar Ridge for a class reunion and to sell her mother's house. She'd thought she'd leave it all behind.

But that was harder than she thought. Especially now that she understood more about her mother's issues and that she had risked her life to protect her. She had her answers.

She'd even confronted Prentice, who was hiding behind his attorneys. Gretta had led the press in an attack on him and revealed that her mother had been victimized.

Stone pulled up in front of the inn and climbed out, his big sexy body sending her heart fluttering and her emotions all over the place.

"Hi," he said as he walked toward her. "Are you ready to leave?"

Was she? She bit her lip. "I'm packed," she said.

"What's happening with your mother's house?"

"I hired a service to clear the debris left from

the fire and whatever was left inside, then demolish what was left. The real estate agent assured me the land would sell better once the ruins of the house were clear." And she'd sleep better once it was gone. "How's Mickey?"

Stone had finally confided about his brother's drinking problem, and she admired his dedication to helping him. She also understood why he'd never leave Briar Ridge.

"He's actually doing better. He came to see me yesterday and told me he's joined AA. He's also been writing and plans to start singing at Blues & Brews. Music always was his passion."

"That's great," Macy said, and meant it. "I remember him playing in a band in high school."

A smile flickered in Stone's eyes. "It was his dream. I'm glad he's coming back to it now."

They stood for a tension-filled moment. She wanted to say more. To tell him how much he meant to her. That part of her didn't want to leave.

But her father hadn't wanted her. What if Stone didn't, either?

"Good luck, Macy," he said in a gruff voice.

"You, too." She stood on tiptoe and kissed his cheek, then he wrapped his arms around her and hugged her tight.

"If you ever need anything…"

"Thanks." She pressed her hand against his cheek, then kissed him again and slid into the car. A muscle ticked in his jaw as he watched her close the door and start the engine.

Macy forced herself not to look back as she

drove away. But memories of the night she'd spent in Stone's arms taunted her as she stopped for gas. She reached inside her purse for her wallet, but her palm brushed over something hard and slick.

She closed her fingers around it and pulled it out, then realized it was a river rock. She smiled as she ran her fingers over it, remembering Stone sharing that his mother left messages on the rocks to leave around town. She narrowed her eyes and read the words he'd written—*Remember me, Macy.*

A myriad of emotions swirled inside her, and she grabbed her credit card, inserted it and filled her gas tank. But as she started the engine, she turned in the opposite direction. Ten minutes later, she found herself at the river, walking along the riverbank, picking up stones and putting them in her pocket. She'd run from Briar Ridge to escape her past. But coming home, facing it and being in Stone's arms was helping her heal.

She rushed back to her car. What the hell was she doing? Her two best friends, her mother and the man she loved were in Briar Ridge.

The storms had passed, and the skies were clear, fluffy white clouds floating across the sky. Summer wildflowers sprang up on the mountainside.

Stone's pickup and squad car were parked in his drive when she arrived. She got out, then walked up to the cabin. But when she knocked, there was no answer.

Suddenly nervous, she peeked through the glass front door and saw him standing outside on the back deck, looking out over the river.

Nerves bunched in her stomach. What if he didn't feel the same way she did?

She started to turn and leave but silently chastised herself. She'd left Briar Ridge out of fear. She'd faced the worst coming back. She couldn't run again.

She confronted dangerous criminals all the time.

She had to have the courage to face the man she loved.

Inhaling a deep breath, she opened the door and entered, then walked to the sliding glass doors, which were ajar. Stone turned to look at her, his eyes sparking with surprise. Then worry.

"Did something happen?" he asked gruffly.

"Yes," she whispered. "I couldn't leave. Everything I love is here."

She slipped the river stone in his hand. His brows arched, then a smile curved his mouth as he read the message of love she'd written.

"I love you, too, Macy," he whispered. He opened his arms and she went into them, then his mouth closed over hers and Macy knew she had finally found the home she'd been looking for all her life.

A home in Stone's loving arms.

* * * * *

*Look for more books in*
USA TODAY *bestselling author Rita Herron's*
*Badge of Courage series coming soon.*

*And if you missed the first title in the series,*
The Secret She Kept
*is available now wherever*
*Harlequin Intrigue books are sold!*

COMING NEXT MONTH FROM

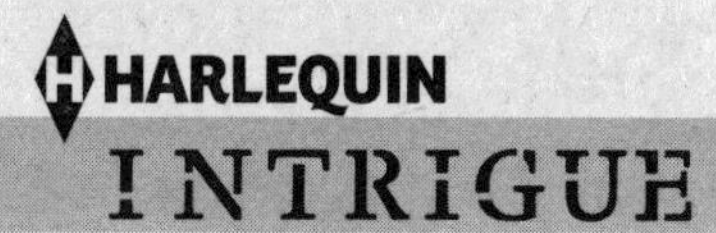


## #2073 STICKING TO HER GUNS

*A Colt Brothers Investigation* • by B.J. Daniels

Tommy Colt is stunned when his childhood best friend—and love—Bella Worthington abruptly announces she's engaged to their old-time nemesis! Knowing her better than anyone, Tommy's convinced something is dangerously wrong. Now Colt Brothers Investigations' newest partner is racing to uncover the truth and ask Bella a certain question...if they survive.

## #2074 FOOTHILLS FIELD SEARCH

*K-9s on Patrol* • by Maggie Wells

When two kids are kidnapped from plain sight, Officer Brady Nichols and his intrepid canine, Winnie, spring into action. Single mother Cassie Whitaker thought she'd left big-city peril behind—until it followed her to Jasper. But can Brady and his K-9 protect Cassie from a stalker who won't take no for an answer?

## #2075 NEWLYWED ASSIGNMENT

*A Ree and Quint Novel* • by Barb Han

Hardheaded ATF legend Quint Casey knows he's playing with fire asking Agent Ree Sheppard to re-up as his undercover wife. To crack a ruthless Houston weapons ring, they must keep the mission—and their explosive chemistry—under control. But Quint's determined need for revenge and Ree's risky moves are putting everything on the line...

## #2076 UNDERCOVER RESCUE

*A North Star Novel Series* • by Nicole Helm

After the husband she thought was dead returns with revenge on his mind, Veronica Shay resolves to confront her secret past—and her old boss, Granger Macmillan, won't let her handle it on her own. But when they fall into a nefarious trap, they'll call in their entire North Star family in order to stay alive...

## #2077 COLD CASE CAPTIVE

*The Saving Kelby Creek Series* • by Tyler Anne Snell

Returning to Kelby Creek only intensifies Detective Lily Howard's guilt at the choice she made years ago to rescue her childhood crush, Anthony Perez, rather than pursue the man abducting his sister. But another teen girl's disappearance offers a chance to work with Ant again—and a tantalizing new lead that could mean inescapable danger...

## #2078 THE HEART-SHAPED MURDERS

*A West Coast Crime Story* • by Denise N. Wheatley

Attacked and left with a partial heart-shaped symbol carved into her chest, forensic investigator Lena Love finds leaving LA to return to her hometown comes with its own danger—like detective David Hudson, the love she left behind. But soon bodies—all marked with the killer's signature heart—are discovered in David's jurisdiction...

---

SPECIAL EXCERPT FROM

HARLEQUIN

INTRIGUE

*Wedding bells and shotgun fire are ringing out in Lonesome, Montana. Read on for another Colt Brothers Investigation novel from* New York Times *bestselling author B.J. Daniels.*

Bella Worthington took a breath and, opening her eyes, finally faced her reflection in the full-length mirror. The wedding dress fit perfectly—just as he'd said it would. While accentuating her curves, the neckline was modest, the drape flattering. As much as she hated to admit it, Fitz had good taste.

The sapphire-and-diamond necklace he'd given her last night gleamed at her throat, bringing out the blue-green of her eyes—also like he'd said it would. He'd thought of everything—right down to the huge pear-shaped diamond engagement ring on her finger. All of it would be sold off before the ink dried on the marriage license—if she let it go that far.

As she studied her reflection, though, she realized this was exactly as he'd planned it. She looked the beautiful bride on her wedding day. No one would be the wiser.

She could hear music and the murmur of voices downstairs. He'd invited the whole town of Lonesome, Montana. She'd watched from the upstairs window as the guests had arrived earlier. He'd wanted an audience for this and now he would have one.

The knock at the door startled her, even though she'd been expecting it. "It's time," said a male voice on the other side. One of Fitz's hired bodyguards, Ronan, was waiting. He would be carrying a weapon under his suit. Security, she'd been told, to keep her safe. A lie.

She listened as Ronan unlocked her door and waited outside, his boss not taking any chances. He had made sure there was no possibility of escape short of shackling her to her bed. Fitz was determined that she find no way out of this. It didn't appear that she had.

In a few moments, she would be escorted downstairs to where her maid of honor and bridesmaids were waiting—all handpicked by her groom. If they'd questioned why they were down there and she was up here, they hadn't asked. He wasn't the kind of man women questioned. At least not more than once.

For another moment, Bella stared at the stranger in the mirror. She didn't have to wonder how she'd gotten to this point in her life. Unfortunately, she knew too well. She'd just never thought Fitz would go this far. Her mistake. He, however, had no idea how far she was willing to go to make sure the wedding never happened.

Taking a breath, she picked up her bouquet from her favorite local flower shop. The bouquet had been a special order delivered earlier. Her hand barely trembled as she lifted the blossoms to her nose for a moment, taking in the sweet scent of the tiny white roses—also his choice. Carefully, she separated the tiny buds, afraid it wouldn't be there.

It took her a few moments to find the long, slim silver blade hidden among the roses and stems. The blade was sharp, and lethal if used correctly. She knew exactly how to use it. She slid it back into the bouquet out of sight. He wouldn't think to check it. She hoped. He'd anticipated her every move and attacked with one of his own. Did she really think he wouldn't be ready for anything?

Making sure the door was still closed, she checked her garter. What she'd tucked under it was still there, safe, at least for the moment.

Another knock at the door. Fitz would be getting impatient and no one wanted that. "Everyone's waiting," Ronan said, tension in his tone. If this didn't go as meticulously planned, there would be hell to pay from his boss. Something else they all knew.

She stepped to the door and opened it, lifting her chin and straightening her spine. Ronan's eyes swept over her with a lusty gaze, but he stepped back as if not all that sure of her. Clearly he'd been warned to be wary of her. Probably just as she'd been warned what would happen if she refused to come down—or worse, made a scene in front of the guests.

At the bottom of the stairs, the room opened and she saw Fitz waiting for her with the person he'd hired to officiate.

He was so confident that he'd backed her into a corner with no way out. He'd always underestimated her. Today would be no different. But he didn't know her as well as he thought. He'd held her prisoner, threatened her, forced her into this dress and this ruse.

But that didn't mean she was going to marry him.

She would kill him first.